MW00809505

■ □ ■ □ ■

DAVID ALBAHARI

David Albahari (signature)

BAIT

*Thank-you for everything
you have done to make
it such a fun year in
youre classroom.
You are the best teacher
I have ever had,*

Translated from the Serbian by Peter Agnone

*Sincerely Edip Yijic
june. 25, 02*

NORTHWESTERN UNIVERSITY PRESS

EVANSTON, ILLINOIS

*P.S.
The author of this book is
my friend. Hope you like it.*

Northwestern University Press
Evanston, Illinois 60208-4210

Originally published in Serbian under the title *Mamac*.
Copyright © 1996 by David Albahari. English translation copyright
© 2001 by Northwestern University Press.
Published 2001. All rights reserved.

Printed in the United States of America

10 9 8 7 6 5 4 3 2 1

ISBN 0-8101-1882-3 (cloth)
ISBN 0-8101-1883-1 (paper)

Library of Congress Cataloging-in-Publication Data

Albahari, David, 1948–
    [Mamac. English]
    Bait / David Albahari ; translated from the Serbian by Peter Agnone.
    p. cm.
    ISBN 0-8101-1882-3 (cloth) — ISBN 0-8101-1883-1 (paper)
    I. Agnone, Peter. II. Title.
    PG1419.1.L335 M3613 2001   2001001064

■ □ ■ □ ■

ACKNOWLEDGMENTS

The author would like to thank the Canada Council for its financial support while he was working on this novel.

■ □ ■ □ ■

BAIT

◼ ◻ ◼ ◻ ◼

"WHERE SHOULD I BEGIN," SAYS MOTHER. AT THE SAME moment I reach out my hand and press the button on the tape recorder. The tape recorder is old. For days I looked in all the stores and inquired where I might purchase such a device; the brand wasn't important. The salesmen were kind; they smiled, they shrugged their shoulders, they showed me the latest models of cassette recorders. One of them, in a shopping center in the northern part of town, admitted to me that he had never seen a tape recorder. He believed, though, that his father, actually his stepfather, had owned such a "gadget." He didn't have a better word for it, he said, because in comparison with today's devices, he said and touched the row of new Japanese models, it can't be said any differently. He gave me his business card. Just in case you change your mind, he said. He remembered the tape reels, too, which he hadn't been allowed to touch, except for the empty ones, of black or colorless plastic, which he had sometimes, that being permitted him, rolled across the floor. All he was certain of, he said, was that his stepfather had constantly listened to Buddy Holly recordings. I put the business card in the breast pocket of my suit jacket. Inside that same jacket, when I'd been preparing to leave, I had arranged my tape recordings. The jacket, folded, had been placed at the top of the suitcase and wouldn't have been able to protect them from a more forceful blow; after all, the cardboard boxes in which they'd been packed would have protected them more, but the sleeves of the jacket, which I had folded across them, after having secured them with elastic bands, had eased the insecurity I felt. I hadn't wished to leave, as I hadn't wished to stay, and the emptiness of the sleeves which embraced the voice transformed into an electromagnetic record could only have added to my indecision; but it was just those two absences that made me lower the lid and close the snap locks. I had folded the list of my things—items of clothing, towels, a few books, sneakers, a toilet kit—and pushed it into my wallet between the papers with addresses and telephone numbers. The tapes hadn't been on the list. I had added them later on, when the suitcase had already been packed. I had packed it on the floor, kneeling, and then I'd straightened up, walked to the bookcase, and from the spot on which they'd been resting since they'd been recorded, behind the volumes of the Academy's *Dictionary of the Serbo-Croatian Language,* I had pulled out the dusty red boxes with the tapes. I hadn't touched them for fourteen years, if I don't count the last time the place was painted, seven years ago, when I removed all the books from the shelves, wiped each one with a soft cloth and shook it out, then stowed them in large boxes stacked in the middle of the room, beneath the chandelier wrapped in a plastic bag. Though I hadn't left beforehand, I had in fact returned for them, I thought to myself as I raised the upper part of the jacket, placed them between the folds of the fabric, and covered them with the folded sleeves. Fourteen years ago, no, sixteen years ago, my father died. He died quickly, in the twinkling of an eye, as my mother used to say, though I was sure he had died slowly, over years, that he had become infected with death the instant when, forty years before, he found himself behind a barbed wire fence in a German camp for captured officers. Mother, of course, denied it. One dies only once, she said, no one walks around like a living corpse. My friends were on her side. You look at history, they said to me, like some romantic, at fate as at a pastoral scene in which, stealthily, evil spirits lurk. No, I said, there are threads that bind a person to crucial moments, when the soul yields, and life after that is only an unwinding of the spool, until the thread reaches its end, becomes taut, and tears out—there are no other words for it—the soul from its worn-out place of residence. The friends dismissed me with a wave of the hand; Mother poured a little more brandy into the glasses and the women brought hot crescent rolls filled with cheese from the kitchen. That was after the funeral. The rabbi had spoken the prayers so softly that the people had risen on tiptoe the better to hear him. The next day, while we were still bumping into each other in the new emptiness of the apartment, I told Mother I wanted to record her biography. I rewind the tape and press the button that says START. "Where should I begin," says Mother, and at the same moment I stop the tape again. I didn't know what to say to her. We sat at the dining room table; in front of me lay the paper on which I had written the day before: "Mother: Life"; in front of her, on a metal tripod entangled in the crocheted tablecloth, stood the microphone; the reels turned futilely, and I stared into her dark-brown eyes, set deep below her brows. I suppose that this silence frightens me now. What frightened me at first, to be sure, were her words. It was two years already I hadn't heard my own language, I wasn't able to hear it often being this far away in the west of Canada, in a city in which everyone is an immigrant, and when it echoed, which is the right word for the little house I live in, from the speakers of the tape recorder, I simply drooped. Had there been more room on the table on which I'd placed the tape recorder, I would have lain my cheek on its smooth surface and promptly fallen asleep. The evening before I had laughed at an old Italian man who said that in the word "Sicily" there are more meanings than in the largest dictionary, and now I was ready to believe that four words that say nothing could tell the story of an entire life. Mother waited; she knew how to wait. Father was the one who had always jumped from his chair and rushed to the telephone, who had started when the front doorbell rang. I drew a six-pointed star, two intersecting triangles, in a corner of the paper. I didn't know what to say to her. I didn't know where things begin, where they end. I had only a feeling of absence and a belief, which I've in the meantime lost, that words can make up for everything. That would have made her happy, that loss of belief in words. Every belief is fine, she said, but he who doesn't know how to keep silent cannot hope to find comfort in words. Whence that look of discomfort on her face as I set up the tape recorder, plugged in the microphone, stretched out the cables. She never wanted to dissemble. She looked people straight in the eyes and showed what she was thinking, what she was feeling, what she was intending to say. Countless times I had tried to do the same, but my eyes always glided off somewhere, my lips pressed together, my face dropped, my brows knitted. Then she said: "Only once did I wish to die, afterward it was easier." I reach out my hand toward the control buttons on the tape recorder. It's not the silence that frightens us but what follows it: the unavoidability of choice, the impossibility of change, the irreversibility of time, the order of things in the universe. The reels begin to turn again. The silence, like everything else in our memories, lasts much shorter. Then, there, I thought that if we continued that way, my supply of tapes wouldn't suffice; now, here, I'm not sure whether at that time I had written anything on the sheet of paper that lay before me. If I had a pencil, I'd try, while the tape is running, to redraw a six-pointed star, or maybe I'd draw a square with a triangle above it, and then a thin spiral, which would change everything into the representation of a house with a chimney, into the shadowy figure I assiduously drew in the margins of books and the corners of notebooks during lectures, at literary readings, during the intermissions of concerts, at business meetings. While the reels turn, some ungreased spindle or dried-out drive belt, as Donald claimed, produces a squeaking noise, quite low, like the squeal of a mouse behind a dresser. The mouse comparison wasn't mine, because I've never heard a mouse, but Donald's, uttered while he was trying to convince me that his old tape recorder was in working condition. We stood in the basement of his parents' house, in a room cluttered with tools, old kitchen appliances, Christmas decorations, and stacks of dusty newspapers, bent over the tape recorder. Quite audible, rather persistent, the sound aroused a doubt in me, I told Donald, that I'd be able to hear my mother's voice. I listened closely, first with my left, then with my right ear. Donald shook his head. That's not thunder making your eardrums ring, he said, but the muffled revolt of the material, nothing more than the squeal of a mouse behind a dresser. Europeans believe so much in doubt, he thought, that they're happiest when they don't have to make a decision. On this continent, he said, whoever doubts remains forever on the bottom or at the beginning, which, at least for the person in question, amounts to the same thing. Donald is a writer. He remembered his tape recorder while, in the restaurant on the wide island in the river, transformed into a city park, I told him about my unsuccessful attempts to find a device on which I could listen to the tapes of my mother's voice. He believed that he still kept it somewhere in the basement of their old family house; in fact, he was sure it was there because his father never threw out anything; everything, as he claimed, can be used again, everything awaits a new moment, which, Donald said, turned out to be true, at least in this case, though he, Donald, had always despised that tape recorder because of the tapes of old Ukrainian songs and church choirs his father had constantly brought into his room and demanded he hear just one more time. My father, I said, never used my tape recorder. Which was, really, one of those little white lies by means of which we manage to survive in life. By means of which I manage to survive in life, I should have said, and thus avoid the big lie of generalization. There is nothing in this world that belongs in equal measure to all people, with the exception, perhaps, of the biological functions. In short, from time to time everyone has to empty a bursting bladder, but no one does this in the same way. My father, for instance, would shiver every time he urinated, but I stood, and stand, quietly, and only occasionally lick my lips. We were equally different in the way we pressed the buttons on the tape recorder: Father did that with his thumb, I employed my index finger. We had bought the tape recorder for an exceptionally reasonable price from a married couple, *gastarbeiters,* who had wished to pay off Father in that way. My father was a physician, a gynecologist, an expert in miscarriages, and as ordinarily occurs, in conception and the care of pregnancy. He was the first to record his own voice, having recited a poem of Vojislav Ilić, and therein lay my little white lie. He demanded to have his own tape, on which he intended to record various professional articles from medical journals, to which he would then listen while relaxing after dinner, which he never did. Here my little white lie ended and turned into a truth. On the other hand, Mother never went near the tape recorder. It took us years to convince her that an electric range is better than a wood stove, that an electric boiler is more practical than one that's heated by fire from slats of wood, newspapers, and little lumps of coal. She possessed an obstinacy that my father, at the time, called "Bosnian stubbornness." When she said "no," that meant "no"; there was no other meaning, no other interpretation, no other reading. Years would have had to pass before she, after having said "no," would say "yes," and even then she remained distrustful, ready to remind us, though without malice, of her original refusal. In essence she had been right. The new appliances quickly went on the blink, the burners, heaters, and fuses burned out, the magnets gave in, limestone settled. The wood stove lasted forever. An entire lifetime wasn't enough to burn away its chamotte plating. There was no reason, Mother thought, to be different. Life is not change, she thought, life is repetition. And only now do I know why she gave in, not actually but deep within herself, which I saw in her tearful eyes, when I brought the microphone closer to her and prepared, despite all her previous refusals, to record her voice. Repetition had ceased, life had become change. I told her I was doing it because of Father, because I hadn't been wise enough to preserve his biography, and that her story would truly fill the emptiness that had remained behind him. Had I told her I was doing it because of her, she would have refused. Nothing was done *because* of her, *for* her; rather she did everything for others. Everything emptied into her, every misfortune and every failure, every grief and every suffering. Donald would say of her that she was like a big lightning rod, that every discharge of the dark energies was transmitted to her, that she projected above us, ready to burn out, just to protect us. I know he would say this because I once heard him liken his mother, or maybe it was his aunt, to an umbrella. She stood over us like an umbrella, he said, and never did a drop of rain dampen our heads. I'll never be able to speak like Donald; I'll never succeed in putting words together that way, such that two words create a third, unspoken, or something beyond words, an image, a meaning that really can't be expressed in words, regardless of which language I use, his or mine. Now I knew where my fear came from. In two years a language can be forgotten; in sixteen it can vanish from the face of the earth, and when it vanishes, we, too, are no longer. A squeaking noise is all that remains. Mother looked at me: The way she pressed her lips together was a sign that she had had, as she herself said, "her say." The tape had been running for some time now; then you could hear the door opening, then someone's loud weeping, then my words: "We'll continue tomorrow." We continued after ten days or so, perhaps not until two weeks had passed. By then the procession of relatives, friends, patients, and neighbors had quite thinned out. More and more often we remained alone, especially in the evenings, but Mother refused my invitations to continue with the recording. Once I even set everything up again, stretched out the cords, secured the microphone on the tripod, but when I pressed the buttons, Mother got up and went into the kitchen. I heard that now as two consecutive raps, resembling a gulping sound, the first one short, brusque, like a reflection of my conviction, the second one somewhat prolonged, distorted, when, not hiding my desperation, I slowly stopped the machine. A third rap, when we had indeed continued with the recording, when Mother had agreed to speak, I didn't hear, or, if it was heard, was lost below the squeaking of ungreased spindles. Mother first cleared her throat, which should have reminded me of how uncomfortable she felt, which I knew, both then and now, especially now, but neither then nor now was I prepared to accept this, although now I understand the horror she had to overcome, not in fear of the unknown device but because of the compulsion I had put her under, forcing her to do that which her entire being opposed: to declare her love, to make a choice regarding it at a moment when she still suffered the pain of losing her true love, that toward my father. Now in the little house that by Canadian standards, and despite its modest size, was a real house, though by European standards, considering the material used for its construction, could only be called a shack, I came to know the insatiability of my selfishness. In forcing her to speak, I wanted her all to myself, to turn her feeling of loss into my feeling of gain. You believe too much in words, Donald said to me on one occasion, and that always hinders someone who writes, even if he's not a writer. Writing is a disbelief in words, he said, in speech, in any possibility of narration, it is truly, he said, a flight from language, and not, as they say, a sinking in language itself. Whoever sinks, he said, drowns, and the writer floats on the surface, on the dividing line between worlds, on the boundary between speech and silence. I wasn't sure I understood what he was talking about. I told him about the tapes of Mother's biography and said that I believed a book could be made from them. Donald only shook his head. We sat in the restaurant on the island in the river, transformed into a large city park, and gazed at the skyscrapers in the center of town. The city was raised on the surrounding hillocks that had once been part of the prairie at the foot of the Canadian Rocky Mountains, and the high-rises were on a flat stretch of land bounded by a narrow river and its still narrower tributary, such that they could be seen from almost any point, no matter where one was located. The spindles began to squeak again, or the drive belt was again catching on some bump, and it seemed as if Mother drew air, that she sipped it between clenched teeth. I thought she would burst into tears, for which I immediately had to blame myself, because she never allowed herself to weep in front of us, at least not over herself. She cried because of others, over others, at funerals or weddings, or in movie theaters, while we still, altogether as a family, went to the movies, especially when we saw *The Violet Seller,* but never because of *herself,* not even when the affront had been direct, the memory painful, the hurt evident. "When the Germans entered Zagreb," said Mother, "they trampled through the flowers and the chocolate." I know that sentence well. It was part of the family history and mythology, and I often heard it during dinner, when Father and Mother, together with their guests, talked of how it was before the war. Now it must be added "before the Second World War," because as I sit here in the little house I've rented from a frail old Chinese woman, there, where I came from, a new war is going on; that is, the old one is ending, unrealized goals are being achieved, as though someone has excerpted the past from a film archive and goaded the actors into continuing the opening scene. But the time we sat beneath the old-fashioned chandelier, the real meaning of that sentence had slipped by me. Mother, still dressed in the black blouse and black skirt, sat unnaturally rigidly, her back pressing against the back of the chair, as if she wanted to escape from the microphone, and I, bent over the tape recorder, gazing at the greenish light of the control lamp, which flickered, widened, and gathered in rhythm with Mother's voice, thought only about the quality of the recording, about the possibility that, because of Mother's resistance and the distance she sat away, the words would not be transformed into a magnetic record, or that, spoken outside the direct range of sensitivity of the microphone's diaphragm, they would become distorted, barely audible, useless. Now, if I only knew how to write, I could toy with the absurd paradox that Mother's scornful words about the Germans had been recorded on a tape recorder and recording tape manufactured in Germany.

She, of course, hadn't uttered them scornfully. For her, history had been a fact, a mallet that with inexorable precision had come down on her, on Mother, whenever it had wanted to, and every expression of scorn, despite the pain and despite the force of the blow, would have been only a confirmation of the defeats she simply hadn't acknowledged. The scorn is only mine, an addition I write in, in the conviction that now, far from the new war, I better understand the old one, though I never understood why someone would want to throw chocolate under the feet of marching soldiers. But while flowers flew through the air and chocolate was transformed into a slimy mess, Mother hurriedly packed her bags. Zagreb was no longer the same city, and Mother's life fell apart the same way mine did when, fifty years later, the new war began and Belgrade became some other city, through which passed, without flowers or chocolate, some other bewildered army. Donald would surely advise me to check the facts regarding the chocolate throwing, so that I don't build on unstable foundations. There is nothing so reliable as history, he said. We sat in the restaurant on the island in the river, nearly in the middle of the park, and he'd earlier, with a polite smile, listened to my idea about turning Mother's biography into a story, perhaps even a book, as I daringly intoned. The daring came from my feeling of loneliness, from the fact, really, that I've always associated writing with loneliness, and that now, after two years on the rim of a prairie, close to the North, I had nothing else but myself. Donald warned me that believing a writer writes in order to save himself from the abyss of solitude is a ruse of writers themselves and, of course, critics, who wish to ascribe to what is merely a craft an aura of superhuman endeavor. Writing, he said, is a search for a proper measure of the relation between the real and the unreal, and when that delicate balance is not achieved, he said, writing turns into idle propaganda, regardless of whether it's a question of the superabundance of reality in socialist realism or the accumulation of the unreal in magic realism. It's for that reason, after all, he said, that it's so difficult to write about history, because it horrifies us with its universality and entices us with all the possibilities that might have unfolded. A bad historical novel, he said, can be written in a day as you sit comfortably in the coolness of a room, *after* the history you're describing has occurred, and you attribute to your heroes the supernatural ability to know that which in real life, in *real* history, they weren't able to know by any means. The way I didn't know that all writers are as honey tongued as Donald. If I didn't write, if I didn't want to write a book about Mother, I'd surely write a book about Donald. I'm sometimes sorry Donald isn't here beside me, not only because of the chocolate under the German boots; but even when that thought kept running through my mind in his presence, I didn't dare let it pass my lips. It wasn't only a question of the respect, the awe, in fact, that I felt toward the writer, as I always have (somewhere deep inside us we tremble before those who are skilled in something that constantly evades us), but also the feeling that Mother's voice, especially now that she is dead, belongs to me alone, in that intimate way in which, for instance, a visit to the grave of a loved one belongs to us. Mother would probably not have agreed. If you're going to grieve for me, she often said, grieve for me when I'm alive, for when I die, it will be all the same to me. However, when Father died, her sorrow was genuine. Like all widows, she went to Belgrade's Jewish cemetery at regular intervals, dusted and cleaned the gravestone, plucked out the grass, and left pebbles, but there was no longer a gleam in her eyes, the quickness had faded from her body, her hands rested constantly in her lap, and if I found her in the bedroom, which was no longer theirs but only hers, I could see that she had simply declined. While we sat in the room and she stubbornly, despite my warnings, moved her head away from the microphone, that was still not apparent: The wound was fresh, the pain unexplored, the absence so real that it more resembled a presence. At length she said: "I was standing at the window and watching people change." I asked her how she'd been able to see that. "They were walking upright, they were speaking in raised voices, their backs were taut, their shoulders square. In Belgrade, when we arrived in Belgrade, people mostly walked with bowed heads, alone or in pairs, and whispered. Every time the children laughed, I had to scold them." I mentioned the fear. "The rabbi asked me that, too," she said, "when I went to him and asked him to convert me to the Jewish faith. 'Don't you see what is happening,' he asked me, 'aren't you afraid?' That was in 1938. I wanted the children to finally know what they were and who they were, and I wanted to finally meet my grandfather and grandmother. I thought of nothing else." She took out a handkerchief and wiped her nose. I, too, take out a handkerchief and wipe my nose. "A hard Bosnian head," my father used to say of her, but with tenderness, as someone might say "doggy" or "kitty," but there was truth in that, just as it was the truth that he had had a soft Jewish head, that he had retreated, not in order to give up but in order to find a new path, while she had remained behind to sit and wait until she had accomplished what she had in mind to do. Her first husband had come from an Orthodox Ashkenazi family, had probably been a leftist, though she never said that, perhaps even a communist, and had contracted with my mother, who wasn't my mother then, for a civil marriage, which at the time, as someone told me much later, could be done in only two places in all of the then Yugoslavia. His parents, who like all real Jews had special dishes for the Sabbath and the holidays, could not accept this. They refused to see their grandchildren until Mother had been immersed in the ritual bath and had shown them a certificate, stamped with the seal of the Belgrade rabbi, that she was no longer called Mara or Maria, but Miriam. The guns were already firing, Hitler was nibbling bits of Europe, and Mother was becoming a Jew in order, as she once said, to clear the matter up. I stop the tape recorder and go into the kitchen, look for the box of crackers, put on water for coffee. Perhaps I'm mistaken when I speak about the political leanings of Mother's first husband. Hadn't he given their younger son the middle name Aleksandar? The first name was Jewish, but the middle one was undoubtedly in praise of the king of the same name, which defined Mother's first husband as a supporter of Yugoslavianism and not as a leftist or communist who cared for the king like last year's snow. That was one of my mother's favorite expressions, that last year's snow. Her speech consisted of a medley of proverbs and sayings, pearls of folk wisdom and fragments of heroic poems, didactic remarks and country witticisms. When I mentioned that to Donald, he said that one could make a style out of that. The writer is style, he said, and if someone doesn't have his own style, then he's only scratching through cold ashes. The water is boiling and I pour it into a cup with instant coffee. I asked Donald how one arrives at one's style. I wasn't sure I had used the right word; perhaps style is found, perhaps it's fought for, perhaps it's won. We sat in the restaurant on the wide, flat island in the river and spoke in half whispers, like conspirators. Donald only dismissed me with a wave of the hand. So long as the writer thinks about style, he said, he doesn't have his own style. Only when he stops thinking about style, he said, will he begin to discern what style truly is, and when style masters him, he said, he will truly begin to write. I couldn't believe my ears. If Donald was right, and I didn't doubt that he was, then the stories in fact write themselves. I still, however, didn't know what style is. I went home, wrote on a sheet of paper "Style: To Find It and Become It," and fastened it to the refrigerator with a little magnetic disk. There it was soon lost under the profusion of other messages I left for myself: announcements of literary readings, want ads, newspaper clippings I intended to send to acquaintances, notices about billing and payment methods for the public utilities, leaflets with the addresses of garbage collection and recycling centers. Mother would never have put up with that. For years she followed us around the house, picked up the things we had strewn about, and stacked them in the dressers. Dishes never sat overnight in our sink. The bed linen was always starched and ironed. Shirts had sharp creases. Socks turned into inverted balls, arranged in rows in the drawers.

When it came her turn to use the silver serving tray, she polished it persistently, until the last dark spot had disappeared. In vain would my sister protest and claim that there was order in her disorder. Mother would bend over and pick up a book, a notebook, a blouse, a glove. From the moment she got up at six in the morning, until she went to bed again, at ten in the evening at the latest, she never stopped working. She was the last to sit at the table, the first to rise, collect the dishes, cutlery, and greasy napkins, to scour away the crumbs, wipe the table. Nothing of that has remained in me. Nothing, in fact, exists in me. Since I've been here, I walk about like an empty shell, like a conch from which reaches the roar of a nonexistent sea. I wear clothes like the heaviest of loads, I bend under the blows of the wind, I'm astonished I have strength enough to hold a cup of coffee. I put it down on the table, beside the tape recorder. I hadn't been satisfied with the way Mother began her story, but I hadn't tried to interfere. "We visited them for the very next holiday," she said. "I don't remember which it was, Sukkoth or Hanukkah, possibly Pesach, but both of them wept. They hugged the children, who also began to cry; then they wiped first the children's cheeks, and then their own. Not once did they look at me. When the war began, they refused to go with us to Serbia. They said no one would touch them in their apartment, that no one had any use for old people like them. They still didn't look at me, not even when they shook hands to say good-bye; even then their glances were directed away from me, at the ground or at the children's faces. And while we were still on the way to Belgrade, they had already been added to the Ustashe's lists of Jews. Then they began to make the same kinds of lists in Belgrade, to take people away to Banjica, to Topovske Šupe, to Sajmište. In the beginning money helped, gold still more, diamonds, too. Later, nothing helped anymore." You became a Serb again, I said. I don't believe I could have said something like that, but I had, and no whining of rusty spindles was able to cancel it. Mother looked at me. If I knew how to write, I would surely describe that look. She said: "No, I never stopped being a Serb, nor did I renounce the Jewish faith then. In war, life is a document. What was written on the paper, and on all my papers, still said that I was a Serb. I registered myself and the children as Serb refugees from the Independent State of Croatia, and we were sent to Kruševac, where they assigned us to one of the nearby villages. I called the boys only by those Serbian middle names, dressed them in inconspicuous clothes, taught them to make the sign of the cross. And the other Jews did the same. We kept our mouths shut, we did the jobs the householders chose for us, we slept where they put us. No one demanded anything of life; life itself was enough for us: milk in the morning, polenta in the evening, a little cheese during the day. We got up and went to bed, and then we got up again." I, too, get up. My life, too, consists of getting up and going to bed and getting up again, and no matter how hard I try, I don't succeed in doing it any differently; in that not even Donald can help me. Mother says: "Sometimes even a little is too much, and it's best not to ask for more." One more sentence whose meaning only now do I completely understand. Mother cleared her throat. The diaphragm on the microphone didn't hold up, the control lamp began to flicker spasmodically, as if it were a heart threatening to stop. I hear myself asking if she wants a glass of water. She pulled a white handkerchief from a sleeve of her black blouse and blew her nose. "All that's from the tears," said Mother. I wasn't sure what she was thinking about. I offered to stop. The spindles were squeaking, the drive belts were groaning, that's how the silence in which we both awaited her answer sounded. Then for the first time I thought about giving up. I looked at her face and repeated to myself: You're causing her pain. Perhaps I should have spoken that sentence. But the voice, said Donald, is not words, the voice is the onomatopoeia of words; real speech is not heard, it is spoken within. I hadn't known that then, while we sat in the room in which everything still reminded one of Father. At that time I wrote long poems in short verse that no one wanted to publish, in which I extolled the incorruptibility of nature and the preciseness of things. My mother's story, the story about my mother, was supposed to change everything. When we finished recording, I packed the tapes in cardboard boxes and put them in the bookcase, from which, if I don't count the last time the place was painted, I never again removed them until, two years ago, I decided to leave. Writing, or rather the idea of writing, has faded in me, like countless other things. I have always started, I have never finished. Not a single collection of poems have I managed to put together, undecided between their sequence and their titles. Mother, of course, was different. Don't leave for tomorrow, she said, what you can do today. If the dishes had to be washed, she'd wash them; if the pita had to be baked, the pita was baked in less than no time. If she hadn't been so, Father, when he returned from the camp, would probably have sunk like a stone thrown in water. Mother was that way: She pulled herself through, dragged herself from, wrenched herself free of every quagmire. If losses may be compared, then theirs had been the same—Father's first wife and their children had been killed in the camp in Niš; Mother's first husband had been shot and their children had died in a train wreck—but Father always looked back, while Mother went forward. Pain exists in order to hurt, she said; nothing can be changed about that. Father only smiled; if she hadn't supported him, he would have surely fallen. "I want to continue," said Mother. I removed my hand from the control buttons of the tape recorder. "But I don't want to speak about hatred. I've never hated anyone. Unhappiness comes when it wants to; nothing can be done about that." Again she raised the handkerchief to her nose, to the corners of her eyes. "Had God wanted it differently, everything would have happened differently. A person follows a road that leads to a place where a new road begins. There are no crossroads and there is no going back. When Belgrade was liberated, the war ended for us. The only thing left to do was to return home, even though I didn't know where home was. For four years I had lived in someone else's home, and the only thing I thought about was my desire to find a place I could call my own. At first I went to Belgrade alone. I carried a can of lard, a small sack of flour—you never knew when they might be needed. Dead soldiers were still lying on some of the sidewalks. There is nothing more horrible than when you have to step over a dead man, but I wasn't always able to walk around them. They were all young, those dead men, even when they had beards. I returned to the village next to Kruševac and said to the children: 'We're going home.' They thought I meant Zagreb, but I hadn't meant anything in particular. I didn't even know whether Zagreb still existed, and even if it did, I would never have returned to it again. There where they once don't love you, they won't love you again, and they probably didn't love you before. I didn't try to explain this to the children; everyone has a right to his own love." And that's how it was: Despite all the losses, only words of admonition passed her lips. History had been the sum total of facts, sentiments had had nothing at all to do with it, and everyone had had to come face-to-face with them: face-to-face with history, face-to-face with facts, and face-to-face with sentiments. An all-inclusive view, a prescribed insight, a ready-made precept that can inform man about the way of the world does not exist, but each must discover for himself both the insight and the precept. Those weren't her words; it is merely my attempt to define her essence. The attempt, of course, is fruitless. When my father died, I realized that we know least about those who are closest to us, and for that reason I tried to get Mother to speak about her life, though, when she died, twelve years later, I had to admit to myself that nothing, at least when it's a question of our knowledge of those closest to us, had changed. True, during their last days, in the hospital or in our apartment, I had seen them naked, carried them, cleaned up their urine and excrement, changed their clothes, touched the wrinkled scrotum and the withered breasts, but that had been only a body, a shell, the necessary armor of the human soul. If I knew how to write, if I knew how to use literary allusions, I could attribute all sorts of things to that nakedness, thread it into the tradition or ascribe to it a universal meaning. Nonsense, my mother would have said, there are no universal meanings, everyone is as naked as the day he was born and everyone shivers for himself in this world. Even if those weren't her words, they would have pleased Donald, I'm sure. I met Donald as soon as I arrived in Canada, by pure chance, as they usually say, though that's utter nonsense, because nothing, not even this, is by chance. I went into a bookstore and asked the salesman for the book that best expresses the vacillation of the Canadian soul. Donald happened to be in the bookstore, overheard my request, and helped the perplexed salesman. He praised the uncommonness of my approach to literature, and so one word led to another and he invited me for a beer. Donald is a writer, I've probably already said that, but I have to repeat it in order to quiet the longing to say the same about myself. I'm not a writer. The poems I once wrote no one has read; even I stopped reading them at one time, though I kept the folder containing the unfinished collection. I suppose that in poetry there should be an exactness of purpose, or a roundabout way, seemingly imprecise, that leads exactly to the purpose, which I've always lacked. That's why, as a reader, I had a predilection for writers whose purpose was unclear or for those, and they were, I think, the best, who didn't have any purpose at all. In that respect, my mother had really been a poet, as my father had been a storyteller. In real life, Mother had been both. When we were small, she read to my sister and me, recited heroic poems, sang love songs, corrected homework assignments. When we were grown, she gave it up. No, she didn't give it up then either. She kept vigil over us like the Yiddish mothers in Jewish jokes; she guided our choices, selected our clothes. The presents we received for our birthdays were always practical: Vujaklija's *Dictionary of Foreign Words and Phrases,* for instance, or Prosveta's *Little Encyclopedia.* But when we started to outgrow our childhood loves, she truly gave it up. Everyone is the blacksmith of his own fate, she said. Only once did I hold a blacksmith's hammer in my hands, and I knew, as my muscles strained futilely, that I would never be able to forge anything. So now I'm sitting here, in the North, watching my life diminish and sizzle like red-hot iron in water. I hope that this comparison is appropriate, that red-hot metal does not betray the frozen embers of the Canadian winter. Donald brought that to my attention. If you write about the desert, he said, don't mention the shimmer of fish scales. My mother talked like that, I answered. We sat in the restaurant on the island in the river, drank beer, and nibbled peanuts. The waitress came and poured fresh coffee into our cups. Two times two is four, said Donald, but it's simply unbelievable how many people there are who don't know how to figure that out. My mother would have agreed. She always knew how much money she had in her pocket, how much in her purse, how much in the dresser drawer in the bedroom. Father brought home the pay, she managed the house account. I never learned those things, neither the ability to earn nor the skill to spend. "And then I sat down with the householders," said Mother, "drew up the total, settled the account, and informed them we were leaving. They offered to let us stay for as long as we liked, but already I was no longer there. The war was over, at least in that place, and from that moment everything was different. When you don't have a choice, you sit and keep quiet, but when the choices open up, then you have to decide for something. I packed in one day, but at least another four or five weeks went by before we were really ready to leave. I went to Belgrade, tried to locate friends, visited the Jewish Community Center, leafed through the first lists of the missing. The emptiness I'd smothered within myself like a snake during the war years reappeared with each name I recognized. So many people had been transformed into a first and a last name, sometimes with a middle initial inserted, that I sometimes had to feel ashamed I was alive. It was the end of December, the last day of the year. When we had to leave for the train station, the oxen refused to approach the tracks. Their master threatened them, flogged them, but they didn't want to move. The boys sat on rugs, quietly, facing each other. That was the last time

I really saw them." She fell silent. I thought she would reach for her handkerchief, but she only sat there and stared at the microphone. And now I expect to hear a sob or the sound of weeping, even though I know she won't utter a sound. Perhaps silence is also a part of style? Because of that I'm sometimes sorry Donald isn't here beside me, though at the same time the question of translation worries me, because he wouldn't understand anything unless I translated Mother's words for him; but then I really wouldn't be able to listen to them, since that kind of translating requires the continual erasing of the previous contents, such that none of what Mother says would be left for me. Perplexity, I suppose, is inevitable for every newcomer, although there are those who associate it with the sign of the zodiac under which one is born. I don't know about anyone else, but as for myself, I know that I never felt perplexed, at least not in the years preceding the civil war. Perhaps, being so far away, I see that in a mistaken light, perhaps I'm adapting memories to new demands, but I remember the certainty, I remember the assurance with which I walked down the street. Here, I walk hunched over and fix my eyes on the ground, always at the spot my left or right foot is supposed to get to. In our old living room, when sitting with Mother, I always pressed my back against the back of the chair, but now I don't even try to find it. I think Mother also sat that way, always tensely, nearly on the edge, almost stooped over, in contrast to Father who longed for the armchair and knew how to relax. If I were more skillful, I could work out that scene in detail, but I lack the words. It's as if I've diminished since no longer speaking my own language. You're worth as many people as the number of languages you know, said my mother, though she herself didn't know any other language well besides her own. I'm speaking about language because exactly it, someone else's language, is constantly telling me I don't belong here, that I'm incapable of precisely expressing abstract concepts in it, condemned to the world of nouns and figures, newspaper banner headlines, and the labels in supermarkets. The biggest problem with writing, but at the same time its greatest attraction, said Donald, is that the writer really always writes about himself. I didn't want to contradict him, but I could have said to him that no one can be that which he is, let alone someone else. "When I saw them again, they were no longer among the living," said Mother. "But then, before we left, when they were sitting, I saw them quite clearly, just as they were and, at the same time, as if they were someone else, as if each of them had two faces. We had already managed somehow to drive the oxen to the railroad car; we had gotten to the station, got on the train. In the compartment with us was another Jewish family. They, too, were returning to Belgrade. 'Suddenly my life has expanded,' the woman said. It's as if I see her now saying those words, with a smile on her face, as if she took pleasure in them, and the first thing I thought of when I regained consciousness after the accident was that sentence: Suddenly my life has expanded. And when the doctor came into the room, he didn't have to tell me anything. I knew everything. I only asked him if I could see them. I buried them in the cemetery in Velika Plana. As I stood before their gravestones, I understood the bitter truth of the words the woman in our compartment had spoken. She had stayed alive, all the others had survived, the only victims had been my two sons, and then my life truly expanded; it came, in fact, to its end and contracted to a point after which, whether I liked it or not, it had to begin expanding. In the meantime, I walked through the streets of Belgrade like a sleepwalker." In the fur coat that would be for her, as for many other prewar women, the only real proof of the existence of another time. The fur coat and an album of photographs, that's all she had kept. Father had had still less, considering that he'd been mobilized at the beginning of the war and then taken to the camp, to Germany, so that his belongings consisted of a few dozen letters, two notebooks in which he had written his daily notes and the verses of Vojislav Ilić, and three or four photographs, by all accounts those he had taken with him into captivity. Mother also had a wad of worthless prewar Yugoslav money. She never allowed us to destroy it, convinced that one day, as she said, things had to change. For all that she didn't think about politics, because politics didn't interest her at all, but about the economic situation, and she repeated that sentence, which could even begin to sound like a threat, whenever prices in the stores started to go sky-high. For her, politics had been summarized in the words of a new prince, new bondage; about the system we were living in she used the expression: The judge accuses, the judge condemns; she herself had been, as she said, "one of Franz Josef's pioneers." I never entirely understood the last claim, but of the numerous interpretations, I was most often inclined to accept the one according to which: a person who had grown fond of the empire, for Mother had in fact been born during the Austro-Hungarian monarchy, could find peace and quiet in no other national creation. If there was any truth in that, then Mother had been constantly on a downward path: from the empire, to the Yugoslav prewar kingdom, to the alleged democracy immediately after the war, to one-party communism. Such sentences, Donald thought, should never be found in a literary work, no matter how exactly they describe some character. I protested and asserted that it was not a question of exactness but of concision. My mother had been born shortly before the fall of a monarchy and the birth of a new country, and for her entire life, perhaps precisely because of that, she wouldn't know to whom she really belonged, which is the most difficult form of belonging. When her new country, Yugoslavia, fell apart in the Second World War, she, as a homeless person who was no one's, could have thought, at least for a moment, at least in my mind, that she was finally free, because the greatest freedom is when you don't belong to anyone, just as, five years later, when the country was restored, she could have thought that the force of history was weaker than ever, which would, forty-five years later, prove to be the biggest illusion of all, and history would leisurely work off the task it had begun a half century before. Donald just couldn't orient himself in that account in which were mixed the historical and grammatical tenses, country and blood, borders and divisions. In short, I said, when Yugoslavia fell apart for the second time, my mother could have died happy, free from having to cling to anything. There wasn't anything anywhere: She was a dream that was living in someone else's dream. She had never had anything, she had never received anything; they had always taken from her, she had always given and lost, and if something *had* existed that she could remember at the end of her life, then that was the unselfish love of two men, of two loves really, separated even at the same moment they had been joined, the first having emptied into the second, the second having emptied into the first, and that was all she was sometimes able to think about: That will protect me. Yes, said Donald, but what is love exactly? I hadn't been prepared for that question. I hadn't, in fact, been prepared for any questions. I had come to that fashionable restaurant on the island in the river solely in order to drink a beer in peace and found myself in the position of having to descant on the essence of human life. If I knew how to write well, I'd describe the anger that seized me at that moment. If I knew how to write, I'd write a book, I wouldn't constantly pester Donald for advice. Donald is a writer, which is why, I suppose, I have so much trust in him. That wouldn't have pleased Mother. Unlike Father, Mother always said that it's better to be mistrustful than well meaning, and while Father received everyone with open arms, Mother knew how to wait, her arms folded across her bosom. Now that I think about it, she always sat that way. One might say she was obstructing the way to her heart. It would be better, however, to say she was blocking the way out of her heart. When she lowered her arms in one's presence, her face also changed; even when I was small I could see a glow on it. When children become people, they stop seeing what they were able to see when they were children, they even begin to doubt it, but that doesn't mean that what they were once able to see no longer exists. One evening, for instance, when I was nine years old, we sat in the darkness in front of the family house in a straggling

Bosnian village, and a whitish glow was scattered from her face. I thought it had something to do with the beams of moonlight, but when I looked up, I caught sight of a still thicker darkness of clouds. And during the recording, first in the living room, then in the bedroom, once even in the kitchen, she occasionally held her arms across her bosom. She said: "I didn't despair, I didn't contemplate the end. I was peaceful. I thought only about how, in order to expand, an emptiness was necessary, and if I had anything, then I had an emptiness. And I constantly walked a little bent forward, as if I were pushing it in front of me. Then I met your father. He had just arrived from the camp, gaunt, diminutive, in a suit he'd gotten from the Americans, with curly gray hair and a sunken face on which everything, save the eyes, was dead. In the beginning he cried constantly. He would put his head on my shoulder and cry, with deep sobs, like a child, as if something had been torn away from him. The rabbi married us, not the one who had converted me to the Jewish faith before the war, but another one, perhaps somewhat younger, though you couldn't tell that by his appearance. Whoever wasn't in a camp was a refugee or was hiding with a friend. It was all the same, the war had left its mark on everyone's face. At that time it was decided your father would go to Peć, where he was to work as a gynecologist in the local hospital. They put us in the house of a Turkish family, in two small rooms on the second floor. And then everyone there was surrounded by high walls, and as I sat in the flickering light of the gas lamp, I had to imagine my life as lost. I constantly wondered whether I wasn't perhaps mistaken, that the woman on the train had nonetheless been right, but in no way did I succeed in finding a trace of that expansion. Two years had to pass before your father got a position in the hospital in Ćuprija, in order for the first cracks in the edifice to appear. By then I'd had my fill of listening to stories out of Serbian and Albanian mouths, and I wished only to leave Kosovo. There where every voice has a double echo, there can be no truth. At the same time, it seemed to me that I had never been happier. Your sister was born, you were born, and at least my body somehow calmed down; and when the body is calm, the soul is peaceful, too." I hear my voice saying that it would be better if we stopped for the day, that Mother was surely tired. "I'm not tired," said Mother. My voice is saying that she is. I recognize the impatience in my tone; I probably should have gone out somewhere. "If it's alright like this," said Mother, "I can talk a little longer." I told her that it was, but that I had to—I paused a little—listen to the tape so that I could prepare new questions. I was probably also staring at the paper on which was still written only: "Mother: Life," although the number of six-pointed stars, smaller and smaller and grouped in the lower right-hand corner, had grown considerably. Now, in a Canadian city, I was disgusted by my readiness to lie to someone who several days before had buried the person closest to her; there, in Zemun, I hadn't been prepared to begin stammering either. "Alright," said Mother and I knew she didn't believe me. Mother got up. I hear the chair squeaking, then the parquet floor creaking under Mother's feet, the door to the room opening and closing. I reached out my hand and stopped the tape recorder. I hear that click again, the moment when the tape recorder is recording on its own, and then the tape continues to wind, though no voice is coming from it. I'm not counting, of course, the squeaking. I rewind the tape, play it again, rewind it again. The continuation of Mother's story is on another tape, though I can't think of one good reason why I didn't continue to use the first tape. The entire past is made up of little acts whose meanings completely escape us. Those are Donald's words, but I'm certain that I, too, once said them, and before he did. In general, it often happens that I feel myself existing simultaneously in many places, in various times, and that I continually repeat the same events. Someone who knows how to write could make a good story out of that. Donald thought that something more was needed for a good story. He didn't say what; I had to encourage him. Heartbreak, said Donald, in every story the heart must break, not only out of love but out of everything because of which it may break, out of passion, for instance, or belief. Where the heart does not break, he thought, the story breaks. I liked all that about the story, even though I didn't know how to explain to myself how it comes to that breaking, what breaks, and where the words go, the English ones or the Serbian ones, it was all the same. Some philosopher once warned that what can most drive a person insane is the belief that he commands language, even though language in reality rules us, something like that. I knew that well during the last two years in Canada, perhaps better than anything else, I knew nothing else so well, I perceived nothing so clearly as that power of language. I felt the other language taking possession of me, adapting me to its requirements, myself becoming another person. And that's why, when I heard Mother's voice, I winced, not because her voice had come, as is commonly said, from the other side of the grave, but because I felt, and that like real pain, how my language was dragging me away from my new host and returning me with great speed to my original form. When I asked Donald, he said that such things shouldn't go into a story. Whoever explains, he thought, takes away from the story. I nevertheless asserted, and I don't know where I'd gotten so much daring from, that a story can be anything, even the absence of a story. We sat in the spacious restaurant on the wide island in the river which, located in the center of the city, drew all its energy into itself. Because of that we always went to the same restaurant, though for Donald that was just one more expression of the European spirit. How do you like that, said Donald; although we're here for only the third time, I'm already being imbued with that decadent European sense of ownership of place. Donald dreamed about Europe in the same way a European dreams about America. I, too, once dreamed about America. And who hasn't? I also told Mother that it would be alright if she related some dream. She refused. In fact, she said: "It doesn't bode well for whomever I dream about." I hear my voice, low and distant, as if I'd been standing in another part of the room, demanding additional explanations. "Everything comes true," said Mother. "When I dream about an illness, then I know that nothing can stop it. When I dream about some person, the next day he is already showing up at our door. And I always know when a letter will arrive." The only letters she had written to me were the ones I received while doing my military service in Banja Luka. In thick, even letters, equally slanted, she told of family happenings, mostly in connection with my father or my sister, while herself she summed up in a single sentence about her health. And when she wrote letters to relatives in Israel and America, she refused to speak about herself. She had, in fact, been a scribe. Father dictated the letters, stretched out in his chair, his eyes closed and his hands folded on his stomach. His handwriting was illegible, and I admired the pharmacists who succeeded in reading the prescriptions written in Father's hand. His dreams I didn't come to know of either. Countless times he had woken us with his screams, and when we'd run into their bedroom, we would find him sobbing in Mother's arms. He never wanted to tell us what he had dreamt. Mother once mentioned his stay in the camp, but on another occasion she spoke about his first wife and children whom the Germans had killed in Niš, and then about his older brother who had perished in Šabac. I could no longer make demands. I remained silent and, judging by the squeaking, I had sat down at the table. "But one does not live on dreams," said Mother. "One can live on everything else, but not on dreams. My late aunt used to say that the best dream is the one that is never dreamt." And in spite of this, she would cut out of *Politika* interesting articles about dreams, along with their interpretations. She cut out other things as well: recipes for dishes, instructions for preparing various potions, little tips for the home, women's trifles, a cartoon here and there. She kept all of that in cracker and cookie boxes, in a closet in the anteroom, and at all times she knew where each of those clippings was located. And not only the clippings but old nails, screws, pieces of string, burnt-out fuses, corks, keys, rolls of wire, everything had its own place, its own box or jar, in the pantry or the anteroom, sometimes on the balcony, and she would always, unerringly, go straight to the item any of us was looking for. When he heard this, Donald began to clap his hands. A few people turned toward our table. That's wonderful, said Donald. According to him, Mother had been an ideal character for a play. You shouldn't contemplate a novel, he thought, because her tale demands a straight-line chronological narrative, or even some kind of interior monologue, and today all novels, even crime novels, are written in fragmentary form or, even, masquerade as something else, as a dictionary or a technical handbook, and such a form, however fragmentary in its essence every life has been, is simply not suitable for her life. I agreed. If I ever write about her, I told Donald, I'll write a stage play. Donald cheered up and ordered another beer. Mother said: "I once asked her: 'How will I know which dream it is?'" The dull thumping is probably the sound of my fingers tapping on the tabletop. "'I'll know,' she told me, 'when I begin to dream it.'" Then she began to cry. She looked for the handkerchief, pulled it from a sleeve of her blouse, wiped her eyes and blew her nose, while I sat and stared at my fingertips. Now, however, I can't sit. I think about stopping the tape, but I get up, take the cup of cold coffee, and go to the window. There's something unpleasant in listening to someone else's crying, not a single view outside the little house in which I live will change this. If listening to the recordings were not of vital importance to the book I may write, I'd immediately go outside, if only into the backyard. That, too, I inherited from her, that sense of honoring commitments, even when the duty was unwanted and the task unpleasant. In the army, therefore, I was popular among the officers and disliked among the soldiers. I wandered through the grounds of the Banja Luka barracks; I used to imagine I was a torch, the flame of a gas lamp in the evening: Some people I attracted and others I repulsed, some people I'd warm and others I'd scorch. The trouble lay in the fact that I didn't demand any kind of compensation for my obedience. I once said to Father: "If you weren't a Jew, you would be the perfect Christian." I sometimes, especially when I was doing my military service, thought this also about myself. I carried one submachine gun, but I was prepared, if need be, to carry two. But, about that time, about that "parody of an army," which is Donald's quite accurate definition, it's tasteless to speak since the moment the civil war began. Until then I had considered comical the fact that for ten months I had carried around a submachine gun without a firing pin, an unusable heap of iron, but since May 1991, if I'm not mistaken, I find that fact tragic, and in a certain sense I blame myself, in the appropriate measure, of course, for what later occurred. Had I been more resourceful or more persistent then, or at least less obedient, and seen to it that the weapons got repaired, it might not have come to all this. In that tiny flaw I should have recognized the crack that could imperil everything, and this indeed came true, for from that crack a chasm grew into which an entire country has fallen. In the mid-1970s, however, when I was in the army, I saw that lapse of the system, which should have worked infallibly, as a gift from heaven to a young man who didn't believe in that system and thus found himself in the situation of being a soldier without real military qualities. In the army, in fact, I dreamed the whole time of being a baker, that my weapons were flour and the wide wooden paddle for loaves of bread. I wrote about that to my parents, and from Mother I received a letter in which, in those thick, even letters, she wrote that in the army one should be a soldier, in a bakery a baker, on the beach a swimmer, in the yard a gardener. I couldn't decide whose expression that was. It certainly wasn't Father's, because his thoughts were more precise and resisted any kind of repeating. Mother knew how to use rhythms, to intertwine several folk narrative phrases, to line up a row of adjectives, to scramble the structure of a sentence, to tell a story. We sat around her captivated, intoxicated with suspense, shrouded by the tangled grapevine, until the darkness would completely blot out our faces. I have never seen darkness so thick as in

Bosnia. Donald thought I was exaggerating, that I was trying to find symbols or explanations for what had happened in Yugoslavia in everything. We sat on the restaurant terrace, which was located almost at the very center of the spacious island in the river. We removed the beer bottles, glasses, saucers, and cups of coffee, stacked them on the chairs, and spread out a map of Europe. I had wanted to bring a map of the Balkans, but I'd barely managed to get a map of Europe. I had waited more than twenty minutes while a rather old Japanese woman, the proprietress of a small bookshop in a nearby shopping center, succeeded in finding one. She crouched among the files and boxes containing the maps and repeated that she was sure she had a new map of Europe, with the borders of the new countries drawn in, but that little pieces of the world are easily misplaced in the many, especially when all the changes of the last several years are kept in mind, about which, she said while still crouching, she didn't know a great deal, but she did know that on some of the maps she had lost about two hundred dollars, because no one had wanted to buy them any longer. No one even buys maps anymore, said Donald, because television is quite all one needs. Most people don't know, he thought, how many continents there are and where they're located, because global knowledge is something that, paradoxically, he thought, doesn't fit into the times we live in, which stress the predominance of the regional. People here, said Donald, shrink from a surplus of knowledge, and the encyclopedic spirit is the spirit of the past. An American or a Canadian knows only what he needs to know, and he considers that to be the meaning of education; that is, knowledge is what affords practical support to everyday living. Our heads were nearly touching above the spread-out map. I was filled with the unpleasant feeling that Donald understood nothing of what I was trying to explain to him. He followed my finger with his eyes; sometimes he stopped me, sometimes he himself touched the map, but I knew he remained aloof, protected by the screen of his Canadian kindness. Never in my life, not even in England, have I heard so many polite phrases and so many thank-you's as in Canada. If I had to choose three things, or perhaps five, that have been the most difficult for me, and still are, since being here, getting used to the inordinate kindness would be one of them. Nothing so much frightens as kindness, nothing so much leads one to suspicion as a smile. Donald considered these to be the thoughts of a lonely man, that solitude sometimes takes away rather than gives, that it leads one astray. My mother, however, had always reproached me for my insecurity. She thought I'd inherited that from Father. It could never happen to her, she said, that she didn't know what she wanted to buy when she went into a store. It wasn't important which store, a grocery store or a fabric shop, it was all the same. She always just went in, got what she wanted, paid for it, and came out, but he would linger beside the display of fabrics, undecided, unsure whether to give priority to the quality of the fabric or the stylishness of the pattern. In the same way, Donald sat beside my map, undecided and unsure, stooped under the profusion of names and historical facts I had heaped on him. Unlike my mother, who had wept composedly. I don't know whether it can be put that way, whether one can truly weep composedly, but neither then, during the recording, nor now, during the listening to it, did I try to ascertain how long it had lasted. I was unable to determine why she was crying, but I was sure it was the first time she was crying that way in front of someone, and I suppose that this, together with the deference I felt toward her outpouring of pain, kept me from stopping the tape recorder. Mother whimpered and sobbed, more and more softly, and I stared at my fingertips and the designs on the table-cloth. I didn't dare raise my hand to scratch myself above an eyebrow. "We can continue," said Mother. I looked at her. I once tried to describe to Donald what I'd seen on that face, but I didn't succeed. In fact, the more I told Donald, the less I succeeded in explaining to him. What seemed to me at first, when I arrived in Canada and met Donald, like the flash of his understanding, with time proved to be his inability to pass from general concepts to individual ones, to replace a global comprehension with an understanding of details. While we talked about Croatians, Serbs, and Muslims, about partisans, Ustashe, and Chetniks, Donald nodded. He knew east from west, as he knew which great powers had fought in the Second World War, but historical islets like the former Yugoslavia, on which the historical plains had interfered and evaded the main course of events, left him completely perplexed, and when something here, on the North American continent, perplexes, a person becomes indifferent at the same moment. I was persistent, though. If I knew how to write, I told Donald, I'd sit down and write a book, but because I don't know how to write, I said, I have to speak. Fine, said Donald. He watched my index finger which slid down the Balkans like a stick through mud. If you don't understand that path, I told him, that descent which was at once real and symbolic, as was that other path, the inner one, on which the soul, while all around it was falling apart, attempted to remain whole, ceaselessly revising itself and changing from one identity to another, then you'll never succeed in understanding not only that woman, my mother, but also everything that makes up that corner of the world, and when only one part of the world escapes our understanding, then the whole world escapes us. I lowered my index finger onto a black dot. Here, I said, in Zagreb, she was first a Serb and later a Jew, in any case a foreigner, a double foreigner, if one can put it that way, but she felt, in spite of everything, that she could belong here. When, after the Germans arrived, the Ustashe came to power, she carried to her first husband, who with the other Jews had gone on a forced cleanup of the streets, lunch in little metal pots. While she waited to eat, she saw an opaque curtain being lowered between her and the world. She became a Serb again and left, together with her husband and two sons, for Serbia. First she went to Derventa, I said and slid my index finger, along the river Sava, to a smaller dot. That was her first step on the path downward. I suppose, I said, that already then she wasn't quite sure what she really was, especially when she was instructing the children no longer to tell anyone they were Jews. She thought that here, near the village of her birth, she would be able to remain, but because of the Ustashe, who had held her several days in a camp, they continued on to Belgrade. Again my index finger sailed the Sava. In Belgrade they moved in with her husband's relatives in Dorćol. I didn't even try to explain to Donald what Dorćol is, at least not then, though I'd once drawn him a rough sketch of Belgrade and Zemun, and the confluence of the Sava and Danube Rivers, and at that time I had surely shaded in the part that, at least approximately, Dorćol takes up. Again they quickly took away her husband on forced labor and to a camp, and Mother continued to descend toward Kruševac, into a wider and wider darkness, into the bowels of a war that was also growing wider and wider. At the time she lived, I'm sure, as someone else, not, of course, under another name, but as if she were living in two places side by side and from one of them observing herself. She didn't know who was observing whom, she only walked, brushed against the hens and the little dog, and wondered whether life would once more, if only for a while, be as it once had been. Then, after the war, after a few months spent in Belgrade, when it seemed she was again beginning to climb upward, despite the ruins and the things that had vanished and the people who had been lost, she literally fell downward to Peć. If we hadn't gotten along so well with the Albanians, she once said, we would never have overcome the power of that darkness. Perhaps Father said that, I'm no longer sure. The war was over in some places, but here, in Kosovo— she felt that in her womb, in the new fruit within her womb— it was only just beginning. The walls were high, the gates narrow, the windows protected by bars. In Belgrade the rabbi married them; not the one who had converted Mother to the Jewish faith before the war but another one, younger, though one can never be sure when it's a question of rabbis, I told Donald, because their faces become wrinkled from constant reading. And when I was born, they took me to Priština to be circumcised, where the last group of Kosovo Jews was slowly melting away and moving out. Donald stopped me. First he gently took me by the index finger. Then he said I wasn't allowed to speak that way, that a story about Mother should be a story about Mother and not about me or anyone else, least of all about me. And he didn't let go of my finger. I always do that, I told him, I always speak about myself when I want to speak about somebody else. Donald released his grip and shook his head. But with Mother it had been different: When she kept silent, I, too, kept silent; when she spoke, I listened. Now, as I return to the table in my room, I regret that I didn't ask her more questions, that I permitted her to find the threads between the little pieces of her life herself, but I had worried about making a mistake somewhere, and I had erred in not recognizing her need for understanding, better said, for additional understanding, for which, even though she'd never have admitted it, she longed after Father's death. In truth, when Father died, something also ceased in her: as if she could no longer endure the assaults of fate and counting the gravestones she had been around to visit. Those are explanations, said Donald, let *her* speak. That was the first time I had seen so much passion in him. "Alright," said Mother, "we came to Ćuprija. I returned to the place where I had spent the war years, not exactly to the same place, but close enough; they were the same people. Your father worked in the hospital; he practiced at home, went twice a week to the clinic in Paraćin, where he performed curettages. He would return late at night, with purple lips, and I would scold him for not having wrapped himself better in the blanket as he rode in the carriage. He would remain silent; he always remained silent, but we never lived with secrets. I spread out my life before him, and his he laid out in front of me. Each of us had had his own loss. He hung a picture of his children on the wall, I carried mine in my wallet. He had only a few photographs, probably the ones he had taken with him when the war began, and all those years I dragged along two fat albums, as if in that way I could preserve my previous life. Sometimes we looked at them together, at first just he and I, and then you two, your sister and you. I didn't want to speak about that at all. Ćuprija is a small place; there was a party hierarchy, but also that other one, everyone knew who was who, and a doctor was a prominent person, not like today. Had we stayed in Israel in 1961, when they offered him a job, perhaps everything could have been different, but it would have been silly of me to explain to him where his real homeland was. No, he wanted to stay in Serbia. And before the war he had, after all, called himself a Serb of the Mosaic faith. Here he once had everything, he said, and then was left without anything; later he got everything back again, and that's why he was staying here, here, where at the same time there was also that which there no longer was." I stop the tape recorder and stretch myself, get up, take two or three steps, tense and relax my muscles. Once I also liked to gaze through the window, but I lived on the square then, in a high-rise, and whenever I'd look, something was going on outside: A woman was crossing the street, a dog was standing on the edge of a sidewalk, the treetops were swaying under the gusts of wind, turn signals were flashing in the dusk. I always regretted not knowing how to write and to note down all those stories that happened daily. And here, which isn't the same "here" as the one Mother mentioned, there is no story, there's nothing even to be seen. The entire city is an outskirt; there's no real center to speak of, there are no squares, there are only intersections and shopping centers. Life is invisible. Although I've lived in this house for almost two years now, I haven't met a single neighbor. I've seen their dogs, actually little dogs rather than dogs; sometimes I purposely went near the fence to get them to bark, but the neighbors never appeared. The fat woman who was hanging clothes one time could have been anybody, a laundress, for example, or a relative from Manitoba. Whenever I'd get up, the newspaper was already in the letterbox. The mailman would come before noon, when I was at work. Every two months an employee from the gas company would leave me a message to leave him a message telling him when he could read and copy down the numbers from the dial on the gas meter. Saturdays at noon, sometimes also on a workday, in the evenings, Jehovah's Witnesses would come. Once somebody tried to sell me tickets for a charitable lottery, and a woman with a baseball cap on her head offered me free samples if I answered a questionnaire about the soups and seasonings I used in my daily diet. We exchanged polite smiles, and then I slowly closed the door. My father, however, would not have judged that too harshly. For him, life had been what is given, what is inescapable and must be accepted, which I, at the time, imagined to be an expression of a force whose origin had been tragedy, not realizing, as I do now, that the hurt caused by tragedy never heals, more precisely, that some emptinesses are never filled. Mother would probably have said the same. Only now do I know how fragile they were, how much each of my estrangements had caused them pain, not opening the wounds but rather the emptiness that no words could fill. Perhaps every road is such when it leads away from one's parents, perhaps the slightest disloyalty also leaves the same impression, but that doesn't relieve my feeling of guilt. Donald became furious again. You Europeans, he said, pretend that you're bunglers, and you constantly imagine that life consists of collecting, like someone who arranges postage stamps in an album. Who collects stamps here? Old people! I enjoyed his anger. It helped me believe, if only for a while, that I was surrounded by people who nevertheless felt, and not to worry about the exaggerated kindness, which was surely one of the three, perhaps five, things I had found most difficult getting used to since arriving in Canada. Mother didn't show anger. She held it inside until it turned into pain and a bilious attack. In the morning she would still be the first one in the kitchen, to light a fire in the stove, to go buy a newspaper, bread, and milk, despite the dark circles under her eyes. She'd also had them while she sat at the living room table, opposite the microphone, though I'm sure the pain hadn't been the same. I press the button on the tape recorder. "We lived in the villa of a prewar industrialist," said Mother. "We were supposed to be their subtenants, but they were really ours. They lived in one room and we lived in all the rest. We shared the kitchen. I felt foolish as I walked through a house that wasn't my own, as if with each step I were breaking off a piece of someone else's bread. And later, in Zemun, while we waited for the house in which we had been promised an apartment to be finished, this house, this apartment, and while we lived in rented temporary rooms, that feeling didn't leave me. But before that, in Ćuprija, I felt something else. I felt how people were becoming hard hearted, how no one any longer trusted anyone else, as if there were no longer any compassion. And there wasn't. Life had been divided into a time before the war and a time without time. Whenever we'd go to the movies, I would come out dazed. Your father would hold on to me, and I'd touch your and your sister's hair, and then my own. So many people were spread out there, somewhere beyond the darkness, that it was unbearable. Your father would merely smile, hold me firmly under the arm and return the greetings of passersby, while my thighs quaked. Perhaps that can't be understood today, perhaps even I no longer understand it, but I imagined then that life would never again be life. Once a month I went to visit the graves of my children, and at that time, alone at the edge of the cemetery, I didn't know what to do, to which god to pray, or to complain, and whether to light candles or put pebbles on their gravestones. In the end I did both one and the other. Had I known a third thing, I would have done that, too, for what is the difference? If the heart knows, it will know what to do; if it doesn't know, there is not a candle that will not go out, there is not a pebble that will not crumble. What did I want to say? Can we stop for a moment?" I hear my voice but don't understand the words. I imagine that the voice of someone who'd been crouching under the table would sound like that, and I certainly hadn't been there. "Fine," said Mother and she got up. She had struck the table with her arm, or knee, perhaps with both her arm and knee, because two dull sounds reached my ears. Again I hear my voice and again I don't understand the words. Donald would find in this who knows what kind of hidden meaning. I bring my ear right next to the speaker of the tape recorder in order to hear Mother's footsteps, the door opening and closing, or at least the coarse rustle of her palm smoothing her skirt, wrinkled from sitting. And while the squeaking of little rubber belts reaches my ears, I know the exact number of steps she had had to take in order to get from the living room to the anteroom, from the anteroom to enter the kitchen. There, I could pass through the entire apartment with my eyes closed and not touch anything. Here, where the place never became my own, regardless of the cramped space of the house, I'm always running into something, looking for electrical switches in places where they're not located, stooping down when I should be standing upright, pushing the door instead of pulling it, turning when I should be going straight ahead. The reels are turning, the tape is becoming taut. I'm tired. "Don't tell me about tiredness," says Mother. I gaze at the tape recorder in astonishment. There was nothing to suggest that we had continued with the recording, that she had returned from the kitchen, that a new day had dawned. A coincidence, Donald would say with a self-confident smile, but he wouldn't be able to convince me. I know what I'd say to him. I'd claim that nothing is coincidental, not even the fact that after sixteen years Mother had answered my unspoken thought. Donald would shake his head. You Europeans, he'd say, always think that life is something more than what can be seen, that behind every mirror there's a parallel world. No, I'd reply, we only believe that not every surface is transparent and that sometimes one must peep behind it in order to find out what lies in the depths. This is what happened: I began to speak about myself in the plural, as if on the hard chair in the restaurant on the island in the river a whole crowd might have been sitting and not just one person. Donald saw in that an additional proof of the difference between Americans and Europeans. An American is always only one, is always alone, thought Donald, and a European, especially if he comes from Eastern Europe, is always only part of a multitude. I didn't want to say anything, nor do I have to have a ready answer for everything. If I knew how to write, I thought, I'd sit down and compose a letter in which I'd explain a few things to him: the arrogance of Americans, for example, and the maturity of Europeans, the reality of our history, for example, and the pathetic way they exist in the uninterrupted present, our sense of wholeness, for example, and their fragmentariness, the readiness of Americans to take, for example, and our devotion to giving. But you shouldn't write about that, Donald said to me when, perhaps that same afternoon, I explained my intention to him. I don't know how many times I have to repeat it, he said, but if you don't have a story, then the story doesn't exist. I was sure that until then he hadn't once said that, at least not in those words. Your story is about your mother, said Donald; your mother is your story and everything else is preaching to the wind. Mother would have surely agreed with that. For her, most people spoke only in order to speak; rare was the person who knew how to keep silent, still fewer were those who truly knew how to speak. Countless times, both as a boy and as a young man, I opened the door to the living room and found Mother and Father keeping silent: Father would be reading one of his professional books or underlining articles in medical journals, Mother would be crocheting or knitting, sewing on buttons, or darning socks. Sometimes she peeled apples and handed him the whitish slices. She could peel an apple in one stroke, such that the peel bobbed above the saucer like a worn-out spring. Not lifting his eyes from the text, Father would accept the offered slice and bring it to his mouth. I sometimes thought that they had nothing to say to each other; later I reasoned that they kept silent so as not to speak too much, but now I'm convinced that they no longer believed in words. Perhaps that's because I myself no longer believe in words, because of the ease with which we portray ourselves as others, as if the whole world exists only in us, in me. And sometimes I attribute everything to tiredness, to the dullness which overcomes me more and more, which replaces every sharpness with a roundness, which makes of a cube a cylinder. "Don't tell me about tiredness," repeated Mother. Nor then, twenty days or so after Father's funeral, did her face soften; the circles under her eyes were still dark, the muscles of her jaw quivered below the wrinkled cheeks. "Only when we moved to Ćuprija," she said, "did I begin to wake with the feeling I could get up whenever I wanted to. Up till then, especially during the war, I thought that I would never rest again, that I would always walk as if I were holding something in my arms, as if something were weighing on my shoulders. And then in Ćuprija a Gypsy woman told me I would feel that way so long as I carried my dead with me. 'The dead are the dead,' she told me, 'nothing can be done about that.' She saw in the cards that I would meet a tall blond man, and from the little coffee cup she read me the illnesses I would suffer: veins, heart, and joints. She guessed them all; the only thing she hadn't seen was the blood pressure. And she told me I must rest more. 'Fatigue is falling from your eyes,' she said to me. She also cast beans, but I could no longer listen to her. For four years, the whole time the war lasted, I dreamt how I would one day have a good sleep, and only when we arrived in Ćuprija did I think that this would really happen. 'Your life has been cut in two,' the Gypsy woman told me, 'as if someone has cut it with a knife.' I gave her a dinar or two, a few eggs, a loaf of bread, and an old shawl. And truly my life had been cut in two and left to gape like an open wound. It was because of this, probably, that I was so tired, as if the blood flowed continuously out of me. When you shave, you have a styptic pencil; you put it on the cut and it's finished, but for that cut there was no remedy. At first I thought only the people were changing; then I realized that the whole world was changing and that it would never again be the same, though I never admitted this to myself. Perhaps also because of that I was so tired, because of that refusal to see the real wound, to admit to myself that there was a wound and that the knife had come down not just once, but had been cutting continually. In Zagreb I saw Germans, in Derventa the

Ustashe interrogated me, in Belgrade there were followers of Ljotić, in Kruševac I met Chetniks, later the partisans appeared, and in Peć I watched them take away the Balists who had been arrested. Even now I don't know where they appeared from, and where they had been before the war began. That, perhaps, has nothing to do with fatigue, but when the Udbashi interrogated me in Ćuprija, I could no longer endure it. Someone had reported us and said that we had gold coins hidden in the house. We had them, that's certainly true, but after having kept them from everyone else, I wasn't about to give the coins to them. They were hidden in the pigsty, under a can of swill. They turned everything upside down but didn't find them. While they walked through the house and yard, I held you in my arms. At noon you started to whine, and I had to nurse you. One of the Udbashi, it's as if I see him now: tall and blond, exactly as the Gypsy woman had described him, asked me to unswaddle you. I put you down on the table and untied your diaper. If you hadn't been so skinny, they would have thought that you'd swallowed them. They stood around the table and watched you kicking your little legs. Your father was white as a sheet and his legs shook so badly that the hair on his head jittered. If he hadn't feared my anger so much, he would have surely brought them among the pigs. He was so good, God forgive his soul, that he couldn't recognize evil. 'If you think I hid them between my breasts,' I said to them, 'you can look there, too.' I seized the topmost button of my blouse, and that blond Udbash blushed and went outside. It was then, in fact, that all the fatigue peeled away from me, and that night, it seems to me, for the first time I slept very well indeed. The Gypsy woman had been right: What the knife has cut off, it has cut off." She fell silent, reached out her hand, took the glass, and swallowed some mineral water. I hear well how she slurps and licks her lips. My father was a doctor and he wielded a scalpel, I told Donald, but my mother butchered poultry on the kitchen terrace. Donald was revolted. Like most Canadians, he thought that concern for animals is sometimes more important than concern for people.

When I told him how, as children, we used to chase after head-less chickens, he almost threw up. When I told him, as we bent over the map, about the Ustashe massacres, he only dismissed me with a wave of the hand. It sometimes crossed my mind, really, to thrash him. I'm exaggerating, of course, because I never, not even as a boy, learned how to fight. If I got into a fight, I got a drubbing. Mother would wipe the blood from my face and say I should have been born a girl. Regardless of the fact that both my father and she had wished for a male child, I would have been happier, she thought, had I been female. At least then, she would say as she applied a wide, cold knife to my bumps, you wouldn't go off to war. Nothing could make her surrender her beliefs. Perhaps she wouldn't live to see another war, she thought, but there was not a generation that would travel the road from the beginning to the end of a lifetime and in so doing not have bombs fall on it. However, when the new war began, she was still alive, and even though she hadn't gone near the battlefields, she became its victim. She withered away in front of the television screen through which passed, first timidly and then more and more self-assuredly, the pictures of demol-ished towns. When in northern Bosnia, near the village of her birth, artillery battles began between what remained of the one-time Yugoslav army and new Muslim-Croat formations, she went to bed and didn't get up again. At night, when I would raise the blanket and remove her nightgown soaked with sweat and urine, she would take hold of my wrists, close her eyes tightly, try to hide her nakedness, and repeat: "Don't, don't!" Had she known how ashamed I was, she could have remained silent. I raised her head, then her back, then her hips, and pulled tight the folds of the clean nightgown. In the morning, when I would enter the room with a cup of tea and the medicines, she would avoid looking me in the eyes, as would I when, at night, under the meager light of the table lamp, I tried not to see her stomach, thighs, the tangled pubic hairs. If it can be said of one that they died at the right moment, I told Donald, then it can be said of her, because she passed away before history, which she thought had ended irretrievably, came back to life in full radiance. If, I said to Donald, radiance is the right word when speaking about history. I would sooner speak, I told him, about darkness. Donald only shook his finger at me. He, of course, had no idea what history is, no matter how hard he had tried to explain it to me. On the North American continent nobody really even knew what history is, and it didn't interest them, now, at the end of the twentieth century, when the future was beginning. It doesn't interest me either, I told Donald in that same restaurant, bent over the map, because I've seen it, I told him, at work. I pulled my index finger across the map, from Belgrade to Banja Luka, along the road I had taken in the spring of 1994, after which I'd made the decision to leave, and for this continent, I told Donald, for this country, where nothing is more than a few weeks old. Donald said he didn't wish to discuss it, and that he understood my irritation as a reliable sign of a newcomer's anxiety, the fear that a person, despite every intention, ceases to be that which he thinks he is. If there weren't that fear—he was being persistent—I wouldn't be trying to hide my anxiety, and extremely unsuccessfully at that, he emphasized, in a story about my mother which, unlike real stories, didn't make heads or tails. He'd nonetheless been right. Whoever doesn't know how to write, like me, is the same as the charlatan who claims he knows how to set a broken bone or a dislocated joint and then only makes the injury worse and renders it incurable. Someone who knows how to write, like Donald, would sit right down and write the story, traversing to boot the shortest possible path from the beginning to the end. Nothing in that story would suggest that anything other than the story exists, and not as is the case with me, with my story, if I would only write it, in which there is everything but a story, and which continually falls apart under the shocks caused by the intrusions of parallel realities. Donald told me that this can be explained by the ability to focus and maintain the attention. Some people, he said, are incapable of doing or following several things at the same time, while others simultaneously listen to the radio, watch television, write a letter, eat dinner, and prepare a lecture they have to deliver to freshmen the following week. I replied that my mother had been one of those people, because she could do all that and still sing at the top of her lungs. Donald asked where she had lectured, and I told him that she had lectured to my father, my sister, and me because we were, in comparison with her, eternal freshmen in the art of living. I don't know where we were when we talked about that, but Mother would have surely agreed with it. She directed our lives as a conductor does a symphony orchestra: She saw everything as a whole but knew well where each individual sound was coming from. And what's more: Her real skill had been invisible, such that it might have seemed to every observer that the conductor was really someone else, my father, for example, or, later, me, when Father died. Donald immediately said that this reminded him of a puppeteer who, hidden from view, pulls the strings above the little stage and colorful backdrop. If I hadn't smacked him then, I would never do so. Donald was surprised by my anger and again he tried to tell me about the difficulties immigrants have in adapting. They are, more exactly, we are, oversensitive; we constantly have the feeling that the ground is disappearing from under our feet or that we are living in rooms with sloping floors, such that we are constantly stumbling and sliding, irretrievably, into dark corners. Alright, the floor in the little house I rented really was a bit sloped, and I had to put little shims of wood under the nightstand and the armchair, but not a single corner had been dark, nor did I ever think I was living in the Valley of the Dead. If I had to blame someone for something, then I was prepared to blame only myself, though I don't know why I'd blame myself for decisions I myself had made; and if I hadn't been able to adapt, then, again, I was the only one to blame and not some governmental system, differences in the culture of everyday living, or, perhaps, the caloric worth of the food I daily, often insufficiently chewed, introduced into my stomach. Of course, there are people who associate every departure, even their own, with treason, and perhaps my mother had also been one of them. Remain and endure, that's how her motto could have read. She hadn't, in fact, left Zagreb on her own account, but in order to protect the children and, even though she knew the hopelessness of that hope, her husband. Had she been alone, she would never have left. Later, of course, she no longer desired to return to that city, which at one time I couldn't understand, and which now, when the vampires of Nazism are raising their heads everywhere, I understand perfectly well. Once they have been sown, the seeds of evil, like every weed, remain forever in the same place, until the ideal conditions for their germination are found again. That's a cliché, said Donald. That's a fact, I shot back. I'm not to blame because history is banal, I said, and because it is made up of dull episodes which, if we exclude the blood, the sweat, and the tears, cannot gratify a single modern spectator, particularly him, I emphasized, for whom blood became real only when it was discovered that it transmits AIDS, who associates sweat with a recreation center, and tears with the soap operas on television. I had wanted to be sarcastic, that's true, and I hope my words had sounded exactly that way to Donald. After that, I didn't see him for several days. I even began to worry a little that I'd gone too far; that is to say, I have never been skilled with words, especially when I've tried to say that which they really didn't express. Here my mother had been right: "If you want to say something," she said, "then say it; if you don't, then shush." Best was he who with the least number of words said the greatest number of things, and worst was he who, despite the many words, succeeded in saying nothing. The first she called speech, the second affectation; the first had a "honey mouth," the second was "running off at the mouth." I suppose I came down somewhere in the middle, which I once considered to be the ideal position, though lately, even after having come close to the war, I am more inclined to believe that the average person can more quickly perish than someone who is located in a frontier region. For that reason, I suppose, I myself had chosen a frontier region for my new place of residence, a city on the edge of a prairie and the rim of the North, where the sun, especially in winter, moved uncertainly and low across the horizon, in the same way as I moved through the city center and the scattered suburbs. Of course, if my mother were alive, I'd still be sitting in our apartment in Zemun or, as I'd done countless times till then, walking beside the Danube and muttering verses under my breath. When Mother died, all that, the Danube, the verses, and the apartment, was suddenly transformed into words without substance, as though by her presence she had given them fullness and reality. That's what I think now, here, far enough away from all the former realities, but there, when she died, I didn't think anything, I did only what the bureaucracy told me; I went from building to building, filled out forms, and picked up certificates. In the hospital they gave me a bag with the things that had remained of her: some clean underwear, white socks, the little towel I had used to wipe her face, a box of chocolate cookies, an unopened container of fruit juice. I had to sign separately for the receipt of her wedding ring, which was packaged in its own envelope on which, in the upper right-hand corner, her name was written. I opened the envelope on the street and held the ring up to the light. On the inside of the band were engraved my father's name and the date of their wedding, one of the winter months of 1945. I crumpled the envelope and threw it into the first trash container I came upon; I put the wedding ring in my trouser pocket. I remembered how, as a boy, things were always falling through a hole in the lining, sliding down my thighs and calves, falling into my socks or shoes, or even, much more often, remaining somewhere behind me, in the grass or on the pavement. When Father died, the apartment was immediately filled with people; when Mother died, no one came, at least not that day. Maybe that's a difference one should talk about, said Donald. Nonsense, I replied, perhaps there's a difference in the way people die, but not in death itself, which makes everything equal. I was beginning to sound even to myself like some petty preacher, but that thought had pleased Donald, more than had, quite surely, our conversations about history and maps. He had had to put so much effort into them to understand who had been with whom and who had been against whom in Yugoslavia during the Second World War, and then during the civil war that was still going on, so much exertion just to recall the names of the various warring groups, that the thought of dying in general, undefined by history or ideology, simply gave him relief, perhaps even delight. But, he immediately warned me, I shouldn't trick myself too much into believing that everyone would be prepared to follow my train of thought, considering that most people are incapable of following their own thoughts, let alone those of others. That warning, he emphasized, of course applied in case I was still thinking about the possibility of setting something down on paper. He said that as if a story is a filled pastry that must be lowered onto a white sheet of paper and then read from the greasy stains. In vain were my resistance, my objection that a straight line does not exist anywhere in nature and that things, at best, occur in spirals. A story must have a beginning and an end, said Donald, but if you think that between those two points you can put in whatever you want, then you are thoroughly mistaken. One cannot be constantly indecisive, he said, and hover between history, chronicle, personal fate, and poetic prattle, and then expect besides, he said, that it will interest someone to a degree sufficient, indeed, to such a large degree, that he would be willing to unravel it all. I was plainly surprised. But, I asked, if I don't write about myself, then why would I write about others? Donald gaped at me. I saw on his face the countless words he hadn't spoken, but I also saw he didn't know the answer. Had he been holding a beer bottle in his hand, he probably would have hit me, but the way it was, with the cup of espresso pressed between his thumb and forefinger, that move didn't strike him, I'm sure, as very appealing. Had he had a knife in his hand, the one my mother used to mention—no, I can't continue the sentence. There's nothing worse than when one imagines life to be a series of possibilities, instead of taking it the way it comes. Now I'm certain that this is exactly what Mother had been trying to teach me her whole life long, and which I've never really learned, but I can't blame her for that because, as a teacher, she quite approached the ideal figure of a teacher; that is, she taught without leaving the slightest trace of the fact that she'd been teaching and she was never present when she should have been absent; and if I now think, cramped against the tape recorder, that my life would have been different had I only heard the advice of the Gypsy fortune-teller sooner, nothing will change if I reproach my mother's voice. Perhaps the only thing I'll be able to do is to tell myself I'm mad because I'm talking to a tape recorder. Someone keeps on the mantelpiece above the hearth an urn with the ashes of a child who has died all too soon or of a beloved spouse, and I keep on the table a tape recorder with a voice that reaches from the other world. A voice, ashes, what's the difference? "From that moment," says Mother, "everything changed, and I no longer had the uncanny feeling I still had limbs. What the knife has cut off, it has cut off, and whoever is disgusted by the stump has nothing but that stump. That's why I said to your father: If we stay here, in Ćuprija, this little town will make earthworms of your children. 'What of it?' he said. That's the kind of man he was: Worms didn't bother him either. I told him that he could live with worms, but that my children were still going to be people. And so, two years later, he managed to get a position in the hospital in Zemun, and when the truck with our belongings finally arrived in front of the building on October 22 Street, where we had rented a temporary room, the stumps stopped hurting me. I wasn't able to explain all that to your father; nor did I try to explain it to him. He would leave in the morning for the hospital, return after two, gulp down the hot soup and eat the meat pie, and immediately afterward throw himself onto the couch—in those days we all had to tiptoe around— and in the afternoon he would rush off to the clinic and return late at night, pale, puffed under the eyes, and sometimes, on the cuffs of his white shirt, or just below the collar, I would find tiny drops of dried blood. We took several more such rooms, always in some old buildings, in apartments filled with old furniture, a smell of mildew, and cobwebs that hung in tatters from the corners, until we finally got our apartment, in a new building on Karageorge Square. That was the city limit then, or, rather, the city beginning, because that way, next to our building, led to Zemun, and all the traffic headed for Vojvodina and farther, to Zagreb, headed for the entire country, in fact, went by our house. There was a constant din of automobiles and trucks, buses and tractors. Sometimes I would stand on the balcony and think: If I take that road and only go straight and don't turn anywhere, I'll arrive in Zagreb. I never wished to go to Zagreb again, but, just the same, I never freed myself from the feeling that I shouldn't be on a road that always reminded me of when I fled, and that perhaps I ought to decide to go to Belgrade anyway, at least to be on the other side of the river, protected from . . ." Her voice disappears, but the reels are still turning. I stoop down and hear myself asking her: "From what?" "Drop it," says Mother, "that's all nonsense." I remember how she waved me away, but I was persistent. "I can't believe you were afraid of something," I said. "I wasn't afraid," she answered sharply, "I only worried that everything might be repeated, that often people can't change into something else, and that evil, once it takes hold of a person, can never be removed again." I leaned on the table and almost at the same instant moved away, afraid it would begin to squeak. "And do you feel that way now?" I asked. "If you're asking me whether I still sleep on my guard, then the answer is that I do." She'd always been the one who heard me returning late at night, and sometimes, in a long nightgown and her hair undone, she would come out to scold me. "But if you're asking me whether I believe all that might be repeated, then I'm not so sure, although I can imagine some other refugees taking that same road, perhaps even in both directions." I laughed. There was so much haughtiness and disbelief in that laugh that now, as I listened to its echo in my little Canadian house, I felt like slapping myself. Of course refugees had again taken the same road, of course everything had been repeated, of course one should sleep on one's guard, and of course I had believed none of it. "And that's why," Mother continued, "when I wasn't yet on the other shore, I did all I could to create another shore. I had seen the people in Serbia during the war and knew that there would never again be peace among them, that many of them would spin like those tin weathercocks on rooftops, and that, if there were something one should yet be afraid of, then that was precisely their readiness to follow anyone who leads them, by hook or by crook. And so, as soon as we arrived in Zemun, we joined the Belgrade Jewish community, not in order that I make you, you and your sister, into real Jews, because almost everyone there was only a little piece of a Jew, a shard of broken pottery, but in order to develop in you, and in myself, a sense of real belonging, in order to find some solid ground, there where everything was sliding or turning into agitated voices. Summers we'd go with them on vacation, to Rovinj or Split, and winters to performances in the community hall, where you and your sister also lit candles for Hanukkah and dressed in costumes for Purim. In those years something was always arriving from the American Jews: clothing and footwear, chocolate, cheese, matzo for Pesach, prayer books that no one wanted to take. It's difficult for me to explain that now, but I felt safe there, I knew that none of what was going on around us could harm us there. I didn't push you two into it, I didn't make demands, because I myself, when I had wished to marry my first husband, had followed my own heart, and that's how I knew that the heart, too, can learn, slowly, to be sure, and with much repeating—I'm talking too much, but that's the way it was." I hear us clearing our throats, first she, then I, and then immediately a silence begins which, a little later, I recognize as the sound of unrecorded tape. I don't know whether I could describe that sound as a sound; it is, after all, muffled by the squeaking of ungreased spindles or decrepit rubber belts;

perhaps I'd do better not to call it by any name or simply to say that Mother got up and left, and that the next day I got a box of new recording tape? Well, in such situations I wish Donald were sitting here beside me and that I could immediately, the moment the doubt begins to swell in me, start asking questions. Whenever I had posed them to him later on, written down on scraps of paper or repeated countless times in my head, they were somehow no longer the same questions. It was as if the story were changing from moment to moment, such that that which hadn't been resolved couldn't be resolved afterward. Is it possible, I asked Donald, that a story really exists only in a single moment, in a given moment of a given present, if it can be put that way, and that, therefore, it can never be repeated, because that present is, after all, unrepeatable, like any other moment in time? I don't believe I would know how to describe that look of Donald's. Admittedly, I, too, had someone recited such a snarled sentence to me, would have thought that something wasn't right with the one who had been able to word it, but since it was I who had worded it, I knew that people always react that way to the simple truths that undermine established simple truths. Each person lives in a fortress surrounded by moats, and no one likes those who attempt to build bridges across these moats. I asked Donald a simple question: Is it possible to tell a story at all? I had in mind the extreme ossification of the temporal structures in which we live, but Donald was appalled because with that, I suspect, I had threatened his conviction that art, as the highest form of human endeavor, exists precisely in order to go beyond those structures, which I hadn't in any event called into doubt. Donald doesn't understand something. Donald thinks that a person without roots is a wonderful thing, because a lack of roots makes absolute freedom possible, which is further linked to the elementary American myths about unrestricted movement. The point in question is, of course, the myths of the immigrants, and not the original beliefs of the American Indians. Donald is able to think that way because he's never had roots of any kind. He doesn't know what it means to have one's own place, to know that this place is one's alone, to return to or to abandon forever. I didn't try to tell him that because I wasn't sure I'd know how to tell him in the right way, just as I wouldn't know how to write it down in the right way. If I knew how to write, I could write a book about Donald. I know that a book can be written about every human being, and that all of them would be of equal value, but yet I somehow think that the one about Donald could be more valuable than the rest, at least for me, which is, of course, ridiculous, for if I write a book so that only I can read it, then why would I write it at all? Sometimes I think it's just as well I don't know how to write, because whenever I think about writing, I am confronted only with questions, never with answers. Perhaps that, too, is a lesson I learned from Mother? One more question I don't know how to answer, I think as I remove the rewound tape, return it to its cardboard box, and then take out the tape marked NUMBER 3, put it on the tape recorder, pull its leader through the magnetic head, and wind it onto the right, empty reel. I've forgotten many things, most of the gestures and nearly all the words that were spoken, I think as I take a sip of thoroughly cold coffee, but I remember exactly when we began recording the third tape. The second tape we recorded seven or eight days after the first, which we had begun to record immediately after the funeral and which we had continued and finished some ten days later; perhaps not until two weeks, or somewhat less, had passed did we start to record the third tape, which was begun the same day we held the monthly commemoration for Father. In the morning we were at the cemetery, in the afternoon in the synagogue, where we brought hardboiled eggs, crescent rolls filled with cheese, and two bottles of brandy as refreshments for the guests after the service, so that in the evening Mother and I remained alone in the apartment. Mother, to my surprise, offered to continue with the recording. I was so surprised that I began to talk her out of doing it, even though I had in fact started for the room in which the tape recorder, microphone, tapes, and cables were.

Then I thought she had something special to say to me, so I stopped talking and then reproached myself for my selfishness and reminded myself that, in spite of everything, I was causing her pain; finally, standing in the hallway with all the recording equipment gathered in my arms, I told her that she had to make a decision, but she only set about removing the things from the table. If that's how it is, I said, I remember those were my exact words, without finishing the sentence, but when I finally pressed the RECORD button, I asked her why she hadn't talked about her childhood and why she had had nothing more to add about the world she had grown up in. "At my age," I hear her saying, "I have nothing more to look for there." I protested. At that time I was reading certain writers, Schulz and Kiš, let's say, and Nabokov, of course, who had based their narrative constructions, intended no doubt only for adults, directly on the world of childhood, and I tried to explain that to her. I talked about that, I see now, for almost fifteen minutes, as if we were recording a tape about my life and not hers, as if books truly represent life, as if any imagined life may be compared with any real one. But Mother didn't give in: If she said "no," it would be "no" forever; there was no magic spell that could change that. After all, in earlier days she hadn't wished to speak about her childhood either, allowing us only to peep into the world from which, we suspected, she had so happily fled. We knew only that there had been so many children in her family that her parents had sent her to live with relatives in Derventa so as to reduce the number of mouths that had to be fed. Had she not gone there, she would never have, many years later, met her first husband. Derventa was one of the gateways to the world, and he used to come there, I suppose, engaged in business, and being tall and refined like that, elegantly dressed but modest, all of which I gathered on the basis of the photographs in Mother's prewar album, he surely must have seemed to her like a being from some imaginary world. And her childhood she boiled down to the scar on her right thigh, which she couldn't hide on the beach, the vestige of a prank, a foolhardy attempt to jump over a fence of sticks, on which she was left to hang until someone ran from the house, removed the pointed branch from her thigh, and later bandaged the wound. Out of such or similar events the aforementioned writers had constructed a complex mythology of an Arcadian childhood, but for my mother there existed only the uneven circle of darkened skin at the spot of the puncture. Something had either happened, she thought, or it hadn't, everything else was unimportant, especially conditional sentences. I think constantly of how she made fun of those who imagined life to be a lesser or greater choice of possibilities. "It's silly enough I buy a lottery ticket," she used to say, "why would I waste my time imagining what would happen if I won?" And so she calmly, on Tuesdays, if I'm not mistaken, leafed through the newspaper searching for the results of the drawing. She never won. If someone were to say to me now that this was because she didn't believe in the possibility of winning, I don't know what I'd do out of rage, for if anyone knew how to believe, then it was she, but she believed in that which was happening and not in that which might have happened. When death occurred, she believed in death, but while life lasted, she believed in life; I don't know if that can be explained in a better way. Of course, if I knew how to write, I could put that another way, too, perhaps with fewer words, though it's never been clear to me whether the value of writing depends on the number of words employed. Donald, I don't know what Donald would say with regard to that, perhaps nothing. Maybe I shouldn't think so much about what he'd say, because in most cases he really doesn't say anything. That wouldn't have pleased Mother, the malice that emanates from the previous sentence. I was unable to defend myself with my feeling of loss, the feeling that, considering I was no longer in my own language, I was continually sliding down a slope, for if anyone were able to speak about loss, then it was she, and yet from her mouth I never heard a tone of malice at anyone's expense. Fine, Donald isn't that way, I say aloud, but the twitching of my right hand, and my left hand, which rhythmically squeezes my left knee, give me away. The voice, however, with which I had addressed Mother had betrayed an anger, quite recognizable despite the squeaking of the little rubber belts or ungreased spindles. Anyone else in my place would have gotten up long ago and looked for the lubricating oil; perhaps he would even, if he didn't find it in the house, have gone to the nearest store. "Alright," I said. My voice even trembled a little, but I could already attribute that to the unadjusted drive system and the tapes, slack from sitting too long. "If you don't want to speak about your childhood," I said, "then tell me whether you were happy." "What do you mean?" asked Mother. "The way I'm saying it," I said, "I don't know if it can be expressed in another way." The rage had ripened in me, I could recognize it even here, in the house that would never be my home, an unwarranted rage, cruel in its impropriety, a rage that came from helplessness, from the realization, I suppose, that a child can never be anything but a child and is ever obliged to acknowledge the power of its parents. I don't know what I'd been doing with my hands then, particularly with the left one, though with my right I'd perhaps been squeezing a pencil. Some people are like that: They don't know what to do with their hands. Mother was different: Her hands rested in her lap, and sometimes, in quiet despair after learning some sad news, she would bring them to her face and press her temples. If she hadn't been so calm, I would have packed the tape recorder, rolled up the cable, and returned the microphone to its plastic box. Now I know the real reason I was enraged: because I believed that art is greater than life, and because it seemed to me that in her words, the ones we had recorded up till then, there was only life, raw material, interesting perhaps to some archivist or historian, but completely worthless for the poet or the prose writer. Of course, I knew, I had even written something about it in a poem, that art springs from life, but for that I considered the exaltation of life to be indispensable, and in the life of my mother, in what she had told me up till then, nothing pointed to the exalted.

How foolish I was, I told Donald, perhaps on the very day we looked at the map of the former Yugoslavia, perhaps a little earlier, but in any case in that same restaurant on the island in the river. I was blind, I told him, I was, in fact, blinded by love toward my father, and I forgot that the blind man, just as Mother often said, sees better in the dark than anyone. Donald promptly took out his little pad and wrote down, so he said, the thought about the blind man. A poem can be written about that, he said. I didn't know how to write poems. In my poems, even when I wrote about decadence or ruin, there was always a source of light. "Happiness is a habit," said Mother, "if that answers your question." I said nothing; one could hear me keeping silent very well. Mother sighed. She knew I was becoming angry, but now, as I listen with clenched teeth, for the first time the thought occurs to me that that had been all the same to her, that the pain at losing her man, my father, who had helped her, but without knowing it, for he had, in fact, believed that she was helping him, not only to step out of the abyss of his personal pain, which threatened to swallow them, but also to find a path that led to certainty, to security, and more than that: to forgiveness—that her pain, therefore, had been greater and more sincere than mine. Perhaps I could express that better, but then I'd have to stop the tape recorder. And what did I know then about pain, about loss? Nothing. At best, although this phrase sounds hopelessly wrong to me when it's a question of pain, I believed that pain is connected with guilt. Someone, I believed, was guilty for my pain. Someone, I believed, was guilty for my father's death. Now I know that the pain should not be sought in others, but that we always carry it along with us, that pain is the center that makes us what we are. That sounds pompous, perhaps pathetic, and it surely wouldn't please Donald. I won't even tell him. And why would I have to tell him everything? Mother cleared her throat; one always clears one's throat after a long silence; and she said: "I was happy when you were born." I opened my mouth to say something, but she stopped me. "I was also happy when your sister was born," she said. "And before the war, I was happy then, too. When I met my first husband, who at the time I didn't know would be my husband, I was happy. And with our children, and when his parents agreed to see us all together, and while I waited for him to return from work, I was happy. And then, when everything started to close up, the happiness stopped. You can't be happy when you see the light fading in the darkness. You can perhaps hope, but hope is not happiness, because you know that what once closes can nevermore be the same, not even when it opens again. I wasn't happy when I married your father. How could I have been happy then, when I no longer hoped? Afterward I grew accustomed to it. I said to him: 'Don't ask anything of me, and I will give you everything I can.' And he understood that. I don't know whether you will understand, but you can't be happy when the past is all you have and when you don't give up your memories. We were living in a world that, however much you talked of a bright future, was only marking time, that, however hard you tried to forget, existed only in order to be remembered, that, however much you claimed we were all alike, only showed how different we were from one another. When we visited Israel for the first time, not one of the people I met spoke of what had taken place before the founding of Israel, before their arrival. Life had begun the moment they left the deck of the ship, or got off the airplane, and stepped onto the soil of Israel. What had been before belonged to another time, to a time that had ended. It hadn't been forgotten, but it simply wasn't mentioned, it was history. And that's the point: Whoever lives with history is not living with life, he's a corpse even when he's alive. Life is gulped with a big spoon or sipped from a small one, but you just can't sit there and look at it. What's in the dish you can eat or not eat, there's no third choice, is there?" She didn't wait for me to answer, and it's a good thing she didn't, because at the time I was constantly reading books about mysticism, Zen Buddhism, matter and antimatter, ordinary and parallel worlds, and had I started to speak, I probably wouldn't have stopped until the tape ran out, perhaps not even then, and what we were recording should have been speaking about her, I think, she should have been speaking about herself, and not I about myself, as should a book, if I succeed in writing one, present her, and in no way me, I'm not one of those who in every photograph jostle their way to the front row. Mother only dismissed me with a wave of the hand and continued: "After that, everything was easy. When you make a choice, all your troubles disappear as if by magic. When you make a decision, that's happiness. With us, people never succeeded in mastering that skill, and always remained undecided, unsure which side to go over to, and so belonged neither to the present nor the past, not to speak of the future. It always seemed to them that one kingdom was nicer than the other, especially the one that was no longer available to them. And I, when I arrived from Israel, stacked everything neatly and found a place for it all. The photographs from the prewar album, I told myself, are only little pieces of special paper that slowly begin to yellow; monuments are pieces of granite or marble that special craftsmen make and that do not grow from our hearts; a letter is like a seal, you can read it until it fades and after that it's not worth anything. Well, you may say now that for such a simple decision I needed an entire fifteen years, and that this is a terribly long time, which is true, but that's only because you live in a time in which, thank God, you aren't faced with such a choice. For you there are no before and after, for you there is only a now, this moment, just as for me, then, in my first marriage, there was only that moment, and I was constantly amazed at the people who talked of how once, in the time of Austria-Hungary, things were fine and peaceful, and how one knew who was who and where one's place was. Life appeared to be a continual mourning for what had passed, for what could no longer return. And when you think this way, then, like some sweet poison, you pass it to all around you. I didn't want you to be like that, neither you nor your sister. Nor did your father want that. If I had suffered pain, if he had suffered pain, then why would you two have to feel any responsibility for that? On account of that we did all we could to come to Belgrade, which already then was swelling like beans in water. A big city liberates, which I'd felt for the first time in Zagreb, regardless of the fact that I would never have wanted to return to it again. In Ćuprija I constantly had the feeling a turban was tightening round my head, in Peć I was happy I could see the sky at all, and only in Belgrade, for the first time after the war, did I truly start to breathe. It's true, we didn't come to Belgrade but to Zemun, and at first, which in fact lasted several years, I thought that nothing had changed, that perhaps instead of a turban I was wearing a kerchief, but that it, too, was squeezing me, and then I realized that they were two parts from the same whole, that they were only apparently disconnected, and that they must one day be joined. But I was never able to forget, I didn't want to forget, that what was joining them was old Sajmište, which was slowly, that could be seen very nicely from the trolley or the bus, becoming the center of that new, great city. Of course, I no longer thought of those who had once been in that place, in the camp, from where they were taken away and shot or entered the gas van, nothing could bring them back anyway, but I couldn't hide my suspicion that that new city, in refusing to note their absence, was in fact demeaning them. I don't know why it had to be that way, but that's how it was. The best thing a person can learn in life is that there are moments when he shouldn't ask questions. You keep silent and remember. What is inside you no one can take away from you; what is outside you is not yours all the same. That's why we never said to you, your sister and you: Look at that place, the person guilty for that is so-and-so. We said only: Look at that place. For what is guilt? And who dares, who truly dares to say who is guilty and who is not?" She fell silent. I suppose she was waiting for my answer, but I didn't know, as I don't know now, how to answer her. If I knew, I probably wouldn't be in this house, in this oversized country that doesn't understand itself in equal measure as my former country hadn't understood itself. Mother would have seen in that a fine living irony: From a country that has broken apart you come to a country that is holding itself together only because it doesn't know how to break apart. And she herself had done something similar and remained in a country that was glued together like an old broken bowl and that had held water until the repairmen left; but before they left, when the water was already flowing in streams, they also smashed that which previously hadn't been broken. That's how I explained history also to Donald as we bent over the map. This was easier than telling him about Chetniks, Ustashe, communists, and the king's government in exile. But here, too, God knows, there is nothing to be told, I said to him, because history, in its final outcome, is always the same story about one's readiness to collaborate and compromise in order to save one's skin or to secure political influence. In most cases, I said, you don't live as you yourself want anyway, but the way somebody else wants you to. In a dictatorship the minority has power over the majority, I said, in a democracy the majority rules over the minority, but everywhere there are those who must live in a way they wouldn't otherwise want to. Donald said that I had been brainwashed by a totalitarian system and that I had lost my feeling for every system of values, and I replied that the illusory equity of democracy had created a system of illusory values in him. It may sound as if we were arguing, but as a matter of fact we were smiling. And why would we argue? I will always be a European, as he will always be a North American, and about this nothing can be changed; we will always remain as different as night and day. Now it occurs to me that one should speak about that as about the difference between dawn and dusk, since we, he as a Canadian and I as a Yugoslav, share a lack of recognizable identity, and that our countries, my former and his still present one, take up border regions on their continents, at least in the visions of those who see themselves as the creators of the shapes of those continents. He is a shady creature from the North, and I am a shady creature from the land of no return, which has stood eccentrically in relation to all the corners of the world and to the center itself. In fact, we are like those twins who don't resemble each other at all, which explains why we are simultaneously attracted and repelled. All in all, when I write a book about Mother, if I ever write a book about Mother, I'll surely write a book also about Donald. Even if I don't write a book about Mother, maybe I ought to write a book about Donald. If Donald didn't exist, perhaps I, too, wouldn't exist; I surely wouldn't exist. A flower is difficult to transplant; you have to provide it with the same conditions, the same moisture in the soil, an equal ratio of mineral contents; and a person, when he relocates, completely changes his environment, which is quite understandable, for if the flower were everywhere the same, then there'd be no need for a change of place, and no one would go to another place simply because it is like the first. In short, Donald was, and is, my gardener. If not for him, I would have wilted long ago. Mother would have understood that because she knew how to nurse flowers. Japanese violets sprouted up quick as lightning under her hands. At one time, many years ago, there were so many flowerpots with Japanese violets in our apartment that we couldn't move about in any other way than by hopping. She attributed that luxuriant growth to her ability to converse with flowers. To me all the violets were the same; the only difference between them was in the color of the flowers, though, if I'm not mistaken, the ones with the white petals predominated, and Mother had a special name for each of them. I don't know how long that could have lasted; namely, I was always uninterested in what was happening in the family itself; now I no longer have anyone to ask. Had I asked her, she would have listened to me. She knew how to listen. Father also knew how to listen, but his eyes would quickly coat over with a shiny film, like the transparent eyelids some birds have, which was a sign that he, not moving forward, was moving backward all the faster, to sink into himself, while Mother never lost her concentration, equally patient as she was stubborn. You can't make a story out of that, repeated Donald. He always got flustered when he

tried to explain to me what makes a story. He always emphasized the inevitability of movement, the necessity of there being
a plot. He scorned writers who employed ruses, especially the
one, he couldn't remember who he was, who claimed that the
writer is really a magician. The universe is perhaps warped in an
incomprehensible way, said Donald, but a story must be clear.
That, too, I wrote down on a scrap of paper and fastened it to
the refrigerator with a magnet, though I didn't have the slightest idea of how, from something that is unclear to me, to make
something that is clear to everyone, myself included. The writer
is like a filter in a coffee machine, thought Donald, and he must,
just like the filter, retain the unneeded grounds and let only the
drippings pass, the fluid, the liquid which is the essence. If the
writer explains, he went on, then he remains in the grounds, he
doesn't succeed in overcoming the paper. That metaphor pleased
him, and for days he was proud of himself. Once he even forced
me to watch how coffee is made, how the water, darker and
darker, dripped into the glass pot, and then he triumphantly
removed the filter with the wet grounds. Another time he
explained in detail his theory that the difference between a
progressive and a backward understanding of the world is contained precisely in one's relation toward coffee grounds, and
that backward peoples also pour the grounds into a cup of coffee. He grinned at me across the table as if he had just discovered the final, all-encompassing theory underlying the entire
universe. Had he told me that in Belgrade I would have immediately abandoned him, but in North America one gets used to
such theories. In such matters every North American is even
more stubborn than my mother. She surely wouldn't have been
so understanding. For her, because she had come from Bosnia,
the drinking of coffee represented the moment when, having
forgotten one's daily cares, one approached the divine, when one
sat right next to the raiment of the Lord. After all, she would say,
the future is contained in the grounds, which meant that the
drinking of such coffee, with the grounds, signified a connecting
of all the temporal segments, that is: Whoever drinks coffee

without the grounds exists only in the present. Donald, when I explained it this way, only dismissed me with a wave of the hand, emphasizing that he found in that one more proof of our obsession with history. The little bit of history he had in his own country he didn't take seriously anyway, as if history were a process that leads in both directions, as if it could be revived and changed, as if it were possible all the Indians and the bison that had been killed would again be found on the rolling prairie. If I ever write a book about Mother, I know now for sure, I'll also write a book about Donald. Every beginning is difficult, my mother used to say; afterward it's always easier, you only have to break the ice. I'd like to hear what she'd say if she saw the ice over here. A person would perhaps be able to break that ice, but that would be both the beginning and the end. After such an effort, it would be quite all the same to him; he would simply wish to lie down in that bluish hole and never get up again. If I could write her letters, no, if there were a purpose in writing her letters, I would ask her what she thinks: Why of all the places on the globe did I choose exactly this one, where the end of one winter and the onset of another are joined by a short and illusory two-month period in which, only with extreme effort, can I recognize spring, summer, and fall? She always knew how to answer difficult questions, even those that wouldn't be articulated. She read me, as is commonly said, like a book. She read all of us like books, Father, my sister, and me. We were like a traveling library, and no book bindings could protect us, though we seldom really wanted to be protected. More often we longed for the opposite: that, if we were already books, she take us and leaf through us, that she tell us how to unravel the plot in which we were playing the major roles. In those days we would go into the kitchen, which was her kingdom (and which no woman of today would accept, such a type as she was vanished long ago and never found itself on the list of endangered and protected species), sit down on the hard chairs or stools, and remain silent, waiting for her to tell us what had escaped our understanding. Father was a physician, a man of science and facts; he knew how the body functions, what the best position of the embryo is in the womb, and where the red and white blood cells come from; my sister studied mathematics and for her everything was concrete abstraction, everything could be expressed, both the stars in the sky and the ants in an underground ant nest, in mathematical equations with innumerable Greek letters; in literature I searched for the same brutal logic that enables an architect to build a house or a mechanic to assemble a motor; and again we all waited submissively to hear her opinion, which defied all logic, or fact, or the law of numbers. In the kitchen it was always warm in the winter and cool in the summer, and we simply couldn't understand how she managed that, even when there wasn't a fire crackling in the stove or when the July heat penetrated through the wide-open balcony door. When she died, in the kitchen it was cold in the winter and hot in the summer; it was of no help at all that in the meantime I'd bought a new electric stove, that I'd put blinds on the windows. Some things we'll never come to know, and in that, I suppose, is hidden the meaning of our existence. That wouldn't please Donald, or maybe it would please him, maybe he'd write that down in his little pad, too, I'm no longer sure. I'm no longer sure of anything as I sit here, already a little stiff, and listen attentively to the voice that reaches across time and beyond life. Father taught me by example, by gesture, with words, as if someone were saying to you: A knife is held like this, shaving cream is prepared like this, this is how you tell a woman you love her, and Mother taught without anything, only by her presence or absence, by silence, without words. I don't know if I'd succeed in explaining that to Donald, I don't know if I've succeeded in explaining it to myself. One should never believe too much the teacher who instructs by means of words, I would say to Donald, for he teaches you that the world can be conceived only when a new construct of that world is made, as if the world, in itself, just won't do. Perhaps that's why I came to the northern point of the compass, because the farther north a person goes, the less he feels the need for any kind of construct, all the more is the world only world, pure and clear in its horrible simplicity. That doesn't mean, of course, that he understands it any better, but only that between him and the world there are fewer and fewer intermediaries. The only thing is that I didn't go far enough, I say aloud, and at the same instant I have to stop the tape recorder because my words begin to sound the same time Mother's do. She was waiting for my answer, and when she saw I had no intention of speaking, that I was hanging my head lower and lower and, probably, doodling on the paper that lay in front of me, she got up, and then sat down again. "When someone passes away," she said, "there are no words that can bring him back." I rewind the tape and listen to that sentence one more time. I think of the family that lived in this house before I moved in. When she handed me the keys, the owner, a frail old Chinese woman, told me that the family had had to return because their son had been killed. She didn't say where they had returned to, where they had come from, how their son had been killed, or why she was telling me at all. She gave me the keys, bowed gently, and left. Now I imagine she had related this to me solely in order that I would better, or more attentively at least, listen to what my mother was saying. One more bit of nonsense, Donald would say, one more senseless attempt to ascribe more meaning to things than they really have. The house had been spotlessly clean, there had even been a spray of wild flowers in the vase on the kitchen table. I rewind the tape again, press the button on the tape recorder. "When someone passes away, there are no words that can bring him back," says Mother. That surely wouldn't have been able to comfort the bereaved Chinese family. I don't know why I think that they, too, were Chinese. Perhaps because of the unopened bags of rice I found in one of the kitchen cabinets? One more bit of nonsense, Donald would say, everybody eats rice today; the strictly national cuisine is a thing of the past; on every menu you can find soy sauce, baklava, hummus, pizza, and kielbasa with sauerkraut; it's not important whether you're in the East or the West, the North or the South. And that's the trouble: To him who says that the cardinal points of the compass are no longer important, the world is no longer important either, just as for him who claims that all people are alike, there are no individuals but only an agitated sea of faceless units, as if people were fish or tomatoes. The North is the North and the South is the South, and he who yearns for the North cannot be transformed into someone in love with the South. That's why I left for the North, because I no longer believe in the South. The heat makes a person mild, forces him to believe in apparitions, in visions experienced on the peak of some mountain or before the entrance to an ascetic's cave. The North does not allow any kind of prolixity; the North demands hardness; the North is the essence of concision. The curse of my former country lies precisely in its having been too near the South, which drove the people to believe in visions and which made the visions fleeting, such that as soon as it seemed to a person that he was holding something in his hands, he would be left without anything, and rather than climbing, he would be falling, plunging into nothingness. A country that is spread out between the four cardinal points of the compass, I told Donald as we leaned over the map, a country such as mine had been, a little in the North, a little in the South, a part in the East, and a part in the West, such a country must fail. And when the centrifugal forces stretch away its regions from its edges, I said and dragged my index finger across Slovenia, Croatia, Serbia, Macedonia, and Montenegro, then the frenzied centripetal forces, left to their own devices, squeeze whatever is in the middle. I pressed my thumb on Bosnia and looked him straight in the eye. Donald smiled and nodded; if I hadn't known him, I would have thought that he'd understood everything. If history were physics, said Donald, we could write it out with the help of formulas and always know its outcome in advance, and thus prevent it, but the trouble lies in the fact that history is not physics. Now he looked me straight in the eye. My mother used to say that all is written in a person's eyes, and that one should never believe the person who avoids another's glance. She said of such people that they had darting eyes, while the troubled had eyes like spinning tops, the eyes of the ill burned like live coals, the eyes of the curious were like augers, and of the frightened like a doe's. She once said to me that my eyes were like dogwood berries. Even today I don't know what dogwood berries look like, but every time I look in the mirror I think of them. Donald has tiny eyes and blinks often, as if they're full of dust. Perhaps I shouldn't believe him either, but if I don't believe him, then what do I have left? "When someone passes away, there are no words that can bring him back," says Mother for the fourth time. My first thought was that she was nonetheless begrudging me because, after Father's death, I was trying to preserve her life story by getting her to speak about herself. I shifted uncomfortably in my chair, pouted my lips, and frowned. All of which was supposed to make it known to her, I hoped, that I was rejecting such an interpretation. After all, wasn't she saying just a moment ago that the meaning of life, no matter how tragic, does not lie in naming the guilty party? I looked at her, frowning thus, across the table. Whatever I had thought till then about literature, I was now ready to defend it, to defend the right of literature to words and thereby to the possibility of yet bringing back him who no longer was. "You shouldn't become angry," said Mother. "I, too, when I was young, believed the world can be described, but then events occurred that defied all description, and I can no longer believe in that." I was at a loss what to say. I was still frowning but felt an expression of embarrassment gradually come over my face. I have never been one of those who can remain angry for long. "There is only one way a person can resist evil," said Mother, "and that is to find a trace of goodness in himself. When you constantly think about who the guilty one is, then you destroy every possibility of goodness in yourself. I'm not saying that one should forget, for forgetfulness is also a kind of guilt, which means that it can lead one astray, but that one shouldn't stop remembering. It was for this reason, after all, that I felt safe in the Jewish community. Had they wanted to think about guilt, the Jews after the war could not have sought restitution anywhere in Yugoslavia, or anywhere in the world, but they stayed. To no one did they say you are guilty, but they simply recorded all the places and all the names of those who had been in those places in their books and albums, and if the moment were ever repeated in which the guilty were to be sought, they would merely take out their lists and show the places, nothing more would be needed." I felt I didn't completely understand what she was talking about, but I didn't know which facial expression would be appropriate to that. Now, however, I understand, and now I know. I even tried to explain that to Donald when he asked me why exactly there, in my country, a war was going on. Because of guilt, I told him. Because there are those, I told him, who claim it's more important to know who is guilty for something that happened in the recent or the distant past; even if new guilty ones are created besides; even if every possibility that one live with only the memory of guilt is destroyed besides. And, of course, I told him, when such people turned to the Jews with the demand that they, as witnesses, name the guilty ones, the Jewish community merely produced the lists of names and places and refused to speak. From the lists it was seen very clearly, I told him, that all those who had participated in the previous war—in the vision of those who were demanding the naming of the guilty, the war that was going on now ought to be taking place, as if it were possible to return to the past—all of them, I told him, with the exception only of the partisans, had killed Jews in that war, and that, therefore, the Jewish community did not believe in the naming of the guilty but rather in the naming of the victims. I sounded even to myself like someone giving a political speech, but that's why I was sure that what I was saying was really getting through to Donald. Donald, that is, believed politicians, not because he thought that they don't lie, but because, he maintained, they don't dare lie too much, for if someone catches them in a lie, then their political careers are over. My experience had been different. I didn't believe politicians because there, where I had lived, I learned that politicians, if need be, merely exchange one lie for another, and that this doesn't affect their careers in the slightest. That was best seen, I told Donald, when the new war began. Such a number of shameless lies, told in such a short time, could not be compared with anything in the history of human dishonor. Donald felt the need to pat me on the shoulder. Canadians, in general, rarely touch each other, but patting on the shoulder is permitted as a form of consolation and understanding. Donald had probably wanted to comfort me; I doubt he had understood me. Indeed, he said, it's natural for the writer to aspire to the truth, even though, he added, that is to some degree absurd, inasmuch as his vocation consists of dealing with fictions, which to an extreme degree still represent some kind of falsehood. In short, he thought I had left because I could no longer endure the pressure of the lies, but I had left, in fact, because I could no longer endure the pressure of the truth. In the spring of 1994, namely, the opportunity arose for me, as a translator for one of the international humanitarian organizations, to travel to Banja Luka. The war was still raging on all fronts, the roads were destroyed and precarious, and we constantly came across checkpoints or obstacles that sent us off in new directions. The slovenly, bearded soldiers carefully looked over our documents, asked for cigarettes, chewed blades of grass, and spat. When we arrived in Derventa, I imagined that Hiroshima had looked that way, and that the lunar landscape still looked that way. We had to look for a tire repairman; in that chaos of war, theirs were the only shops that were always open. My mother claimed that in her time the members of fourteen nationalities had lived in Derventa; she had even repeated that to me just two or three months before her death, when I hadn't imagined I'd be taking that trip at all. I never verified her claim because even if there hadn't been fourteen but nine, or only five, and even if it had been a question of some other place, Bijeljina, for example, or Brčko, nothing would have changed in what she had wanted to say with that claim. I asked the mechanic, who, tucked beneath our car, was tightening some bolts and banging with a hammer on an axle, who lives here now. No one, he said, only our people. The representatives of the humanitarian organization wanted to know what we were talking about. The mechanic pulled himself from under the car, wiped his hands on his greasy military pants, and said to tell them that here, not far from his shop, immediately after the war they were going to build the church with the highest bell tower in the Balkans. He didn't know, however, where the dance hall in which my mother had met her first husband had once been located. And if it did exist, he said, the wind was surely blowing through it now. He looked up at the roof of the workshop and we all followed his glance upward with our eyes. Holes everywhere through which the sky could be seen. The representatives of the humanitarian organization asked if they could photograph the workshop, the riddled roof and shattered windows. They had hitherto photographed without asking, from the car, while moving. And later, up till we arrived in Banja Luka, they didn't lower their cameras, or they'd lower them only long enough to change the film, to put in new batteries. Before we left, they wanted to find out why nearly all the houses in nearly all the villages we passed through had been burned down. As far as the eye could reach, on all the surrounding hills, we saw only burned buildings, said one of them. The mechanic looked at them and asked me whether I had told them about the church with the highest bell tower. When I affirmed that I had, he asked me to repeat it to them. When I repeated it, he told me to tell them one more time. If we continue this way, I thought, we'll never get to Banja Luka. The mechanic was satisfied. Those foreigners, he said, you have to tell them the same thing a couple of times, otherwise they don't understand a thing. In a corner of the workshop, leaning against a wall, stood a glinting submachine gun. And then, when we arrived in Banja Luka together with the dusk, the first thing they did was to take us to a vacant square on which, they told us, they would rebuild a church the Ustashe had destroyed in the previous war, forcing the Jews to remove the bricks and building material. I don't know if it really happened that way, though it was also no longer important. I was a translator and not an interpreter of history; history here had, after all, ceased to exist; that is, there now existed some posthistorical time that was supposed to repeat some other time, as if life were a textbook from which they could tear out individual pages and replace them with new ones, which were really the old ones. And then the translators themselves appeared upon the earthly terrain when the Tower of Babel was pulled down, which perhaps hadn't been a real church or temple, but which had surely wished to reach to the Lord himself. God, I read somewhere, is said to have feared that humans, if they spoke only one language, would be able to achieve much more than he had imagined, if he had imagined anything at all, and so he caused there to be a great confusion of tongues, and thus created the need for intermediaries. We were already on the way to Belgrade, not, to be sure, on the same road by which we had come, for owing to the renewed fighting in the vicinity of the Posavina Corridor, we had had to take a roundabout way; and as we bounded over bumps and gritted grains of dust between our teeth, I thought that my country, too, was falling apart because someone, though it would be better if I used that word in the plural, had been annoyed by the fact that everyone spoke the same language. For that reason God had destroyed the Tower of Babel, and here, in my country, they were blowing up mosques, setting fire to monasteries, razing churches. If God was satisfied when he saw what he had done, then it is difficult to deny such satisfaction to others. I didn't even try to explain this to the representatives of the international humanitarian organization, but had I tried, they would have looked at me with the same incomprehension with which Donald looked at me when, pulling my index finger across the map, I finished the story about my difficult trip. We arrived in Belgrade; that same evening I submitted my resignation and ended my career as a translator, and the very next morning I stood in line in front of the Canadian Embassy. With regard I had still believed in that common language, I told Donald; I had been transformed into a prehistoric man; I had been living in a history that no longer existed, in a time that everyone said was not taking place. For such a person there is nothing left to do, I told him, but to go into voluntary exile and thus outwit those who would send him there by force. Exile, when all is said and done, is just another name for the truth, I told him, though it's possible to claim, I added, that it expresses our permanent condition, for Adam and Eve were driven from the Garden of Eden when they learned the truth. My mother, I believe, would have agreed with such an explanation, but Donald was stubborn. He thought that I was loosely accepting, and still more loosely reinterpreting, that was his word, the biblical allegories, and that Adam and Eve had been forced to leave Paradise not because of the truth but because of their disobedience. That's the point we had come to: In the restaurant on the island in the river, over coffee and beer, we were discussing the meaning of the ancient texts, about which, the truth be told, neither he nor I knew a great deal. Something like that would not have happened to my mother. She never, unlike most people I have met, talked about what she didn't know, which I, obviously, haven't learned. What she did know, regardless of whether it concerned the preparation of foods for the winter or the use of the so-called old wives' remedies, she could defend to the last drop of blood, and when she didn't know something, she would say so loudly enough for all to hear. She could not, for instance, understand that someone was prepared to die for his dreams or ideals, but she honored the deaths of those who hadn't been prepared to deny what they had seen with their own eyes. The world was either a fact or it wasn't, no third possibility could be conceived. Therefore she didn't believe in angels, devils, dwarfs, and witches. I suppose she didn't believe in God either, though she never said that. She said something else: that after everything she had experienced in her life—these were her words: after all the crises she had weathered—

she could believe only in her own two hands. And if she said that she feared God quite a little, she immediately went on to say that she feared the government not at all. Not even that did I learn from her, but, like Father, I was afraid of every encounter with the police, customs inspectors, or tax officials. I would really feel my knees shake and, even when I was taller than they, I always somehow looked at them from below. Mother was able to go to the president of the community and pound her fist on his desk. For her that was nothing; for us that was an act of mythic proportions. Although she never became incensed, everyone in our house feared her anger, which I can now explain only as an expression of respect, for she never raised her voice at my sister and me. I don't know where that fear came from, that fear of a person whom every animal would come up to, a dog or a cat in a house, an ox or a goat in a village, even the sparrows would peck from her hand, countless times I had seen that for myself. Not to mention people. She had only to sit and wait; she didn't have to seek out anyone, the others would always find her. That skill I haven't mastered either; rather I have always gone toward people, greeted them with open arms or remained silent in the expectation they would recognize me. About this, in fact, I had wanted to tell Donald. About how we never know enough about those who are closest to us, how we always cross great distances in search of teachers but don't turn to those who are so near us that our shadow is always touching them. Donald would surely say to me that a teacher is always connected with the light, but I know now, squeezed in this little Canadian house, that true learning also may be acquired in the absence of light. If the ancient books are to be believed, God created the day, but he created the night as well and never said that one was better than the other. I could say that to Donald, but then we'd once more find ourselves in a discussion about matters we don't understand very well. Neither is he a true Christian, nor am I a true Jew. Both of us, in fact, are floating on the surface of life, even though stories about how we are seizing it in its fruitful abundance constantly gush from our mouths. Had I known how to learn from Mother, I would know that this abundance is acquired when one simply lives life, I wouldn't keep passing it through a sieve like worm-eaten flour, I wouldn't rummage through it like a child who slowly picks through its plate and removes the tendons from the white meat of a chicken. Now, of course, it's too late. I'm sitting in a house on the edge of a city, in a country that, as mine once did, finds sense in constantly affirming its senselessness and awaiting the moment when it will collapse into itself, infinitely far from everything that once made me what I am, or what I could have been, or what I was. And that chaos of grammatical tenses confirms to what extent I find myself outside life, in which only the present tense exists and there is no grammar. I feel like saying that to the tape recorder, to offer it as a reply to its incessant squeaking. That voice, that squeaking of a voice, is the only real voice in this room: Mother's voice is an illusion, a tangle of magnetic records, and my voice doesn't exist, my voice is mute, I've been keeping quiet for a long time now. From time to time I raise the cup and take a sip of cold coffee, sometimes I stand up and take a few steps, sometimes I stretch myself, and that is all. Even when on the street, or in a bus, or, as most often happens, in some shopping center, I meet the noisy immigrants from my former country and am enveloped in the softness of their Bosnian pronunciation, the drawl of Vojvodina or any of the mimical forms of my language, I don't utter a sound; I remain silent; sometimes I just walk behind them; they are usually a man and wife with two children, dressed, if it's winter, too warmly for a shopping center and not warmly enough for the outside temperature, ill humored if it's summer because of the dry heat outdoors and frightened of the piercing cold produced by the air conditioners, and so I follow them; I go from store to store, uninterested in what they are really saying because it is mostly shouts of warning directed at the children or malicious comments about the quality of the merchandise here, but I am eager to drown in that sea of sounds; only in it am I able to feel natural. Not one of their words managed to reach me, but that's why each of their voices was also mine, and I formed my lips mutely, moved my tongue, prepared a hum of the vocal cords, adjusted the resonance of the oral cavity. On one occasion, as I stood not far from a married couple who, judging by their speech, came from Serbia proper, I saw my reflection in a mirror to the side of a store window. If I hadn't known that that was me, and if I hadn't known what I was trying to accomplish with those puffed-up cheeks, pouting lips, and jutting chin, I would have thought I was looking at a disturbed person. Then my gaze in the mirror met the wife's; for a moment I thought she would recognize in me a stranger who was closer to her than the other people in that shopping center, and I opened my eyes still wider, but she only nudged her husband with her elbow, and the husband, I guess it was her husband, unwillingly tore away his eyes from the black ice skates, or maybe they were black boots, and caught sight of my face in the mirror. And so we stood, lined up in front of the store window, nearly touching, and we looked at each other, existing only in the reflections of some other worlds. They didn't attempt to look at me in the flesh. I saw the husband's lips moving as he whispered something into his wife's ear, him taking her under the arm, them leaving. When I turned around they were no longer there. If I hadn't shouted out in my own language then, I would never have uttered another word, I told Donald. That's how I am, I told him; I hesitate, I vacillate, but when I make a decision, nothing can make me change my mind. That's how I left Yugoslavia, that's how I came to Canada, and if I'm here, then I quite surely can't be there. One can die in a language just as one does in real life, I told him, and if I've already died, and I have died, then I don't have the slightest wish to be a vampire or a ghost and to wander the expanses of that language like some forlorn creature from the tales of Edgar Allan Poe. I immediately, at that time, thought of Mother, of her voice which, wound up in the old tape recordings jammed into the sleeves of my suit jacket, I had carried in a large suitcase. The tapes were the only impractical items I had brought to Canada; everything else in that suitcase had a precisely determined purpose; nothing had been surplus or a useless trinket, if we don't count among them several books, though of the four of them, two of which had been dictionaries and one an illustrated guide across the Rocky Mountains, only the Bible, in the Daničić and Karadžić translation, could be found in the same category with the tapes. I must add to that a little Buddhist bell, a gift from a friend who is probably still somewhere in India, and which has such a sweet tone that it is always capable of—it's enough I ring it only once—dispelling gloomy thoughts and even warding off fatigue. After all, I hadn't carried it in the suitcase but in my pocket, and I have never doubted its practicality. While traveling toward Canada and changing planes, each time before passing through a security checkpoint, I would take the little bell and other items from my pockets and leave them on the metal trays of various colors, and one of the customs officials or policemen would take the little metal ring on its top with his thumb and forefinger and give it a good shake. The tolling of the bell would resound through the airport corridors, the clerks and travelers would begin to smile, someone would immediately say how wonderful the bell was, someone else would ask me where I'm from, a third would already be beginning a story about a similar sound she'd heard on the shore of a lake, and soon everyone would be talking at the same time and passing the little bell from hand to hand, and I'd just stand there and think how I was missing an opportunity to smuggle something in, a hundred grams of hashish, for instance, or some prohibited agricultural product, nothing special; just enough to prove to myself that I could overcome my fear of people in uniform. But when the little bell would finally get back to me, my forehead would be beaded with perspiration, as if in my pocket I really did have narcotics or a stack of picture postcards for pedophiles or a bug that could destroy a yearly crop of potatoes, so that my relief when the customs official or policeman waved me past was real and the feeling of freedom more complete than it really should have been. That's how I exited from the last airport, too, with the suitcase and traveling bag in my arms, and I rode into the city with the feeling that I didn't have to, if that's what I wanted, speak in my own language ever again. I don't know why I swooped down on language; I could have chosen something else: national foods or the Belgrade press, for instance, all of which I could have easily renounced, but when I climbed into the taxi, the moment, in fact, I dictated the address of the hotel to the taxi driver in another language, I thought I would never again speak in my own. The taxi driver was a Hindu, and who knows, had I told him that, perhaps he would have understood me. Donald hadn't. He considered that to be a wonderful way to speed up the process of integration, for a person to feel as soon as possible like a fish in water, which, of course, Donald emphasized, didn't mean that he would immediately find people of his own kind. Sometimes I think Donald sees in me the reflection of a European to whom, considering he is unadapted to North American standards, things must be repeated three times: descriptively, directly, and metaphorically; the order isn't important. That's what our conversations amount to, regardless of where we happen to be, and while I venture to remark that giving up a language represents one of the quicker forms of death, he talks about the advantages of the lifestyle here, about the healthy diet and the sporting spirit, about the open space that makes everyone equal because it gives to all as much as they desire to take. I suppose Donald believes that Europeans think that way about America and Canada, as of an open space whose beauty fills to overflowing the beings of those who surrender to it. If I had more friends, I would have abandoned him long ago, so much do his words sometimes infuriate me. I once told him that his attitude angered me, but he merely smiled and replied that anger is a typical trait of the European, unaccustomed to being told the truth, unaccustomed, that is, to the fact that here, everyone has the unconditional freedom to say whatever he likes. After what has happened in my former country, I told him, I've learned to fear such freedom, because for freedom to exist it must be limited somewhere, I said, and when it remains unlimited it's really not freedom at all but a constant disputing over what freedom is, which saps the energy of the individual, that moral individual upon whose survival the survival of freedom itself depends. Donald, as he had several times before, said that I was crazy, but that he understood this to be a consequence of a life under circumstances in which freedom was an unattainable category, in which life itself was some kind of dream, vision, or nightmare. And your mother's life, he said, was always like that, wasn't it? I didn't know what to say to him. I hadn't known what to say to her, either. "I thought," I say at last and hear myself well taking a deep breath, "I thought we would talk about other things." Mother didn't hide her surprise; she even, quite gently to be sure, struck the table with the flat of her hand. "What have we been doing, then, till now?" I turned my head toward the window and said: "You didn't understand me, you didn't understand me at all." I can't listen to it any longer. First I stop the tape; then I press the button for fast rewind. Up till the end of that tape, I'm quite sure, we had carried on a conversation about what understanding is and whether anything can be understood at all, given the imperfection of language as a conveyer of our images and meanings. The part concerning language had, of course, been mine, and I took up, I'm quite sure of that, too, most of the time remaining on the tape. I showered Mother with various interpretations of the silence and inadequacy of language; one moment I even went into another room to look for a quotation, the patter of footsteps and the creaking of the parquet floor are clearly heard in the recording despite the hissing of the worn-out rubber belts, and when I returned, she, not lifting her eyes, said that life, if it could be told in words, would no longer have to be lived, one would merely need to state it. I should have held my tongue then, but I couldn't help myself. All at once I became a spokesman for the power of words, I praised language to high heaven, I recalled literary works that had changed mankind, writers who had transformed the souls of their peoples, poems that had distilled time and place, I choked on my own sentences, on an eloquence that intended nothing else—I don't have to listen to the tape again in order to hear it—but to insult, to hurt, and, however much I'm disgusted by that now, to humiliate. As the tape slowly turned and the water quivered in the glass on the saucer, I imagined myself hovering over her like some kind of exalted intellect, like some kind of supernatural being above a wretched creature of the earth whom even the explosion of consonants from my lips affected like star-studded fireworks. I don't know why I behaved that way; the shame I now feel is the same as the shame I felt already that evening and which the following morning became almost unbearable; for days I didn't dare look her in the eyes. I suppose I wanted to state my triumph over a life whose abundance, I thought then, consisted of emptiness, of absence, of continual attempts to hold the disunited parts together, whereas my life would be, and had been already, a reflection of fullness, an accumulation of presence, a steadfast ascending, pure spirit. What I truly realized that evening was something else: It was an insight into the ease with which we can exceed every limit in ourselves, turn love into hatred and calm acceptance into bitter anger. And what I felt was not triumph but fear, fear of the fact that life is nothing but a straw in the winds of history and that, no matter what I did, I could do nothing to change this. Then, sixteen years ago, I lived in a time and a society for which history was a textbook, an anthology composed of dead letters and retouched photographs, and the present only an unavoidable step before the entrance to a better tomorrow. It's easy to be prudent today, but I'd be lying if I said that I hadn't been infected with a belief in a brilliant tomorrow. I recognized, like many, the backdrop in front of which the system was playing its performance, but that hadn't affected my feeling of hope, and as used to be said at the time, of optimism about life. In short, I had still believed in the freedom of the individual to create his own world, and what Mother was telling me confirmed that the individual lives in a world in which, regardless of the political system, any aspect of freedom is practically unattainable, in which, as in the Greek tragedies, the individual serves the gods and higher powers for leisure or, what is perhaps the most accurate expression, to kill time. I had pounced on Mother as if she'd been the only one to blame for that, but in fact, I'm well aware of it now, I hadn't dared come face-to-face with myself. It's always easier to create a new lie than to accept a new truth. I remove the tape from the tape recorder, return it to its box, stand up, and turn on the light. I could just as well have sat in the dark; often, in fact, I sit in the dark and observe the lighted street along which no one passes. A man's character is judged by the company he keeps, my mother would have said, but try as I might, I cannot see myself as a participant in so solitary a way of life. That's the point, said Donald when we spoke about that, or about something similar, in the restaurant on the wide island in the river. Once you've gotten drunk on a place's blood, he said, then it's hard to get accustomed to another drink and another place. Had I not been drinking beer, I would have had to order a glass of water to wash the taste of Donald's words from my mouth. I took a sip of beer that way, then tipped my glass and drank the rest to the last drop. There is no way to describe the slowness with which I did all this. During that time, within myself I left Donald several times and returned to him just as many times, only somewhat faster. You cling to Donald like a drunkard to a fence, my mother would have said. And she would have been right, only I'm not drunk, or dazed, I'm simply bewildered, astonished at the speed with which the ground is disappearing from under my feet, regardless of where I'm standing. Most often it seems to me that I'm not standing but sliding, and that my knees would actually begin to buckle. At first Donald thought I needed vitamin supplements; then he claimed that the air in the house I live in was too dry; finally he wanted to take me swimming and on an extended walking tour of the surrounding hills and mountains. One encounter with a bear on a forest trail, he claimed, would change my life completely. You have to go out into nature, he told me, in order to enter yourself, you have to turn yourself inside out like a glove, like a sock from which you remove a little ball of crumpled thread. Donald is a writer and he loves such images: Simple, everyday things best describe the ascent and decline of the soul. I have never achieved such self-confidence in my poems. For me a line of poetry was an iron lever; it had to be solid and heavy, to lift if need be, and to pull downward if need be. Some people simplicity calms and others it upsets, in that lies the whole truth. I don't know whether I can associate that with my mother, but if I compare her with my father, then Father, perhaps like all fathers, becomes hopelessly complicated, always at the farthest remove from the best path, while Mother passes through the labyrinth like a knife through a head of cabbage, without resistance, until it reaches the heart. Everything, in the long run, comes down to the heart, everything always leads to the heart, and the labyrinth, the straight line, the spiral, the circle, all are contained in the same anticipating of a new heartbeat, up till the moment when there no longer is a new heartbeat and when, if we wish to be frank, that is no longer so important to us. I can say that now, but when Father died, and then when Mother died, I couldn't prevent a feeling of ruin, I couldn't prevent a feeling of loss, I couldn't prevent anything, not even the words that constantly repeated themselves in me and tried to tell me how I shouldn't attach too much meaning to that. Of course, every departure is a slow dying, but as I was packing, each item I took in my hands spoke to me of life. All the items had been new, the shirts, undershirts, drawers, trousers, the sneakers I'd bought the day before, nothing was supposed to remind, to have another meaning, to be other than it was. And then, when the suit jacket was already lying at the top of the suitcase, I went to the bookcase, opened it, and took the tape recordings. Donald, when I told him all this, might at least have said that in those tapes I had brought the imprint of a previous life, but he immediately mentioned death instead, rested his arms on the table and loudly, very loudly, said that my problem was contained precisely therein, and not only my problem but that of all those who arrive, and bringing what they should have left behind them, are only marching in place instead of moving forward. A few heads turned toward us. We were sitting in the restaurant on the wide island in the river, and as he frowningly regarded me, it seemed to me that life was indeed slowly leaking from me, drop by drop. Had I only dared withdraw my gaze from him and peep under my chair, I would have surely seen a little puddle. At that time I still didn't know him well and, frightened I might lose him, I didn't dare contradict him. I can imagine how my mother would have shaken her head at that. For her, friendship was always an equal measure of give and take, and when someone set conditions, she said, you could hang the cat by its tail so far as that friendship was concerned. We never had either a she-cat or a tomcat; our house pet had been a dog, and among the dogs we owned, not one had had a long tail. I think about this as I take the fourth tape from its box. If I don't remember some tail, I think, language will irretrievably lose every link with reality, it will remain, as it probably always has, merely a semblance of reality, an image of how the world may appear and not what the world really is. Donald would surely laugh at such a conclusion. He would find in it, I'm sure, one more confirmation of the unbridgeable differences between us. You Europeans, he would say, still think that the world hasn't been discovered yet, that it exists, as in fairy tales, behind seven mountains and seven seas, and that you reach it only after countless trials, poisoned apples, nine-headed dragons, and one-eyed giants. You sit and stare at the spider web, but you don't see the spider that strung it all up. He really said that once, when we went down to the toilet together after the fifth or sixth beer. He even made me close my eyes and sniff the air, in order to force me to convince myself that there, but for the toilet itself and the urine that ran down the curve of the urinal, nothing any longer existed. As I, with my eyes open again, shook off the last drops, I replied that there are people, in India and elsewhere, who drink their own urine, convinced that they can extend their lives that way, which demonstrates, I said, that for them reality doesn't stop at the stench and the excretions but is only then just beginning. If anything exists behind this toilet, answered Donald buttoning his trousers, more exactly, under it, then it's a sewage system or, maybe, a septic tank, only that, nothing more; there are no netherworlds, there is no hell, no black river across which lame boatmen ferry dead souls. I remained silent. Perhaps this can be explained in another way, too, he said. For instance, he said, if someone wants to write a book about his mother, then he has to write about his mother, and if he wants to write about love, then he'll write about love; one cannot, he said, depict a balloon and then claim it's all about the moon. He stared at me with his tiny eyes and blinked. Had he been able at the time to draw a balloon and the moon for me, had he had a piece of paper and some kind of pencil, he would have surely done that. Had he had a little more paper, maybe he would even have written me a whole book, and if I hadn't turned and left, we'd probably be hanging around in that toilet even today, the footsteps of the merry waitresses resounding above our heads. Later, especially when we sat over the map of the former Yugoslavia and my index finger was transformed into a fingerpost, the suspicion returned to me that this was, perhaps, what I was really trying to do, that I was in fact attempting to force Donald to write down what I was relating to him. If I succeeded in that, I thought, if I got him to record my history as if it were his own, then I would free myself from the heaviest of all ballasts, then I would be free. Freedom is all in the head, said my mother, and chains can shackle only what a person allows to be shackled. She had uttered that sentence in the same room, beneath the same old-fashioned chandelier, in the same spot she'd been located when we recorded our tapes, but some ten years earlier. She hadn't repeated it when we actually recorded her life story, though I'd secretly hoped for that, and on one of the sheets of paper, next to the multitude of Jewish stars and assorted triangles, I had written the word "freedom" and

appended a question mark to it. Afterward, since time was passing and the tapes were being filled with other words and with
silence, I had slowly crossed it out, letter by letter, until nothing had remained of it. I don't doubt Donald would begin to
applaud if I told him that, but why would I have to tell him
everything? It's easiest to understand after the fact, said my
mother, and, with frightful precision, this came true most completely when the civil war began. Suddenly everyone knew what
the real meaning of the past had been, but no one noticed that
the future was no longer being talked about, nor even the present, that it was not a question of a psychoanalytical reliving
of some event in order to establish its true sense, but that the
past, life in the past, was being offered in exchange for life in
the present, that a life already lived through was being designated the only genuine life; that is, life was being asked to be a
constant marking of time, a continual reenactment of the past,
which becomes merely an end in itself. When I'd turn on the
television or put on the radio, whenever I'd open a newspaper
or leaf through a weekly, I could always hear or see someone
convincing me that the events of the past were more important than any form of reality I could confront, and that, if I
didn't accept that "understanding after the fact," I would be
choosing life in a void. As if we aren't already living in a void, I
said to Mother as we sat in front of the television, but already
then death was approaching her in strides and she had no words
left to say. She only kept silent and shook her head. Don't stop
talking now, I said, but even had she been able, or wanted, to
talk, none of the bombastic sentences of the television announcers, made up of the same words they always read from the thick
stacks of multicolored papers, would have been heard from her.
In the morning and evening I prepared herbal teas for Mother;
at noon I would steam a little rice and vegetables; sometimes
I would include toasted bread with it all. When Father was
dying, we couldn't stop the torrent of speech from his mouth.
He, who had always said nothing, choked on the words he
could no longer catch up to to say, but Mother, who used to

pass easily from words into poems and back again into words, sat in silence, pressing together her lips and hands, sealed like a document in safekeeping. And now, as I put the last tape on the tape recorder, I can see her, in a dark skirt and dark-blue blouse, her eyes almost completely covered with a whitish film, lost in the armchair that had once disappeared before the presence of her body. "Look at these hands," she said at almost the same instant I pressed the button on the tape recorder, as if she could hardly wait to begin speaking. For days before I had avoided meeting her in the living room or the kitchen, tormented by a feeling of shame ever since the moment we had finished recording the previous tape. Never had the space of our apartment seemed so small to me and never had I moved under the pressure of so great a weight, as if I were bearing on my back my deceased father and on my chest my mother, curled up in a black robe. Then one day she stopped at the door to my room. In her hand she held a glass of water. I pretended not to notice her, that the books on the top shelf suddenly interested me. She turned, went to the dining room table, put down the glass on the tablecloth of starched white lace, and sat on the chair she always sat on during the recording. She had known how to wait, it wasn't worth putting off any longer. I bent down and pulled the tape recorder from under the dresser. I took a new tape, the same little tape that's turning now, though only a moment earlier, while pretending not to see her, I had considered recording the continuation of our conversation on the reverse side of one of the already-used tapes. I don't know why we spoke about the reverse side of the tape when a tape recorder always records on the same side, only in opposite directions. For Donald, I suppose, that would be one more confirmation of the imprecision of language, a proof of how facilely, and carelessly, we use words. Mother began to speak as soon as I had stretched out the cables, set up the microphone, and pressed the RECORD button. "Look at these hands," she said and showed me her palms. I looked at them. "I can't believe," she said, "that I once held all of you in them. I can't believe that I held anything in them at all." The screeching noise that over-powered the squeak of spindles and little rubber belts was prob-ably part of my unintended cry. A cry of protest, of course, for if in our house things had fallen out of someone's hands, then that someone was me; dishes would slip from my hands as I dried them and plunge to the concrete floor in the kitchen, as every glass on the edge of the table, full or empty, inexorably attracted my sister's elbow, and forks and knives, or a demitasse of coffee, fell between Father's fingers. Father was sometimes so clumsy that we wondered how he managed to perform gyne-cological operations, to hold newborn babies and hand them to the midwives. Mother was always the one who said that, after all the things she had lived through in her life, she could still believe only in her own two hands, which we accepted as an irrefutable truth, believing in her hands more than she did herself. The compresses she prepared from a mixture of vine-gar and garlic succeeded in drawing every temperature and fever from our bodies only because at the same time her hands had touched our foreheads or cheeks. When we prepared compresses of the same mixture, we would always, just in case, also take an aspirin. And now she was spreading those same hands as if to show them to the microphone, as if the microphone were a film camera, as if the microphone were supposed to see. "Look at these fingers," said Mother, "look at how they're twisted, how the wrists are swollen. Look at these palms. Feel how the skin on them has become hard." She leaned toward the table, the table began to squeak, the tape recorded that alright, and she held out her left palm to me. I hesitated; it was the first time since Father's death something was approaching me so closely; then I touched it on the fingertips. "I wouldn't dare put it on your face," said Mother, "you'd think it's sandpaper." I said nothing; I hear myself remaining silent. Mother again leaned back in her chair. "That's the story of my life," she said, "gnarled fingers and a coarse palm." I was afraid that she, too, would fall silent. "There are those who can't say even that much about their own lives," I said. Mother, like a magician, pulled a handkerchief from her sleeve. "My first husband," she said, "always said that life is measured according to how much we have done for others." She touched her eyes with the handkerchief, wiped the corners of her mouth, then put it back in her sleeve. "Do you think I didn't believe him?" She didn't wait for me to answer. "I believed him, what else could I have done? When I met him, I still hadn't begun to count the years, that's how young I was. Probably because of that he was 'organized,' as it used to be said, because of that belief that one has to do for others in order to do for oneself. I never asked what kind of organization it was. When it came his turn to hold the meeting in our apartment, I would take the older son by the hand, put the younger one in the stroller, and go out in front of the house. Sometimes I would go to the park and wait for two hours to pass. After two hours I dared to return. In the rooms there was a smell of tobacco, soiled dishes had been carelessly stacked in the sink, books and papers still lay on the table and chairs. The boys shouted and ran about the apartment, the older one opened the windows and the terrace door, but they didn't touch anything. Boys, when they're small, you can teach them everything; you only have to speak to them constantly, to show them how things work. Boys learn by listening, girls learn by watching; afterward that remains with them for their entire lives. My first husband, however, didn't listen. I watched and I spoke, but he didn't want to stop, he didn't want to hear. Whoever isn't for himself, I said to him, isn't for others either. He would smile and say I sounded like some old Jewish wise man. When he realized he had been wrong, it was too late. Not one of those whom he thought he had helped was able to help him, and those who could didn't want to. Life becomes frightfully simple at certain moments, so simple that I have always asked myself: Why all its earlier complexity, why its precautions and vacillations, why its hesitations, when the fall is always so easy, so headlong, stripped of every uncertainty? They took him away twice: the first time in Zagreb, on forced labor, the second time in Belgrade, to a camp. Both times he offered me his hand, he didn't embrace me. His hand slipped out of mine, and had I wanted to, I wouldn't have managed to hold on to it. Later, in a short letter on a wrinkled sheet of business stationery, he wrote me that he had begun to dream with open eyes. Every dream is the same, he wrote; in every dream you open the door and I enter. That door, I knew, would never open again. When once life begins to slide downward, nothing can stop it. When things begin to fall out, they have to break." She fell silent, raised the glass, and took a sip of water; one can hear well how the bottom of the glass strikes the surface of the table. I didn't know what she was talking about; in fact, I didn't believe that any kind of letters existed until, several days after the funeral, I found them in her old prewar handbag, hidden in the dresser, behind the sheets, quilted slipcovers, and pillowcases. There were six of them, more exactly five letters and a short message, written out in Latin characters, with a lead pencil, most often on business stationery, though one had been written on sheets with widely spaced lines, pulled from a school notebook. The message, according to the date in the lower left-hand corner, was written on 23 October 1941, probably immediately after Mother's first husband had been taken to the camp. The first letter bears the date 26 October, while the last one, on the sheets from the notebook, was written on 14 November. On all of them, next to the date, he writes "in the camp." The letters display a mix of quickly written practical advice, expressions of deep and tragic feelings, and a slow realization of the course of development of his fate. The advice concerned what to sell and to whom, from whom to borrow and to whom to repay money, what to do in order to make possible his release from the camp. Love emerges from each of those many-folded pages, and only here and there does one get an intimation of the anger he felt at his own helplessness, expressed in a mild accusation or a sarcastic sigh, quite understandable, I would say, for the situation in which the man found himself. No measure of understanding helps here: The horror in his soul, whose presence one also feels, cannot be described by any means, just as the horror that seized me as I read the letters, with the knowledge of what had happened when the words stopped, cannot be described. I don't know why I hadn't relistened to the tapes of Mother's confession then. Possibly because of the sense of hurriedness caused by the rapid growth of the war in Bosnia. When Father died, for months we didn't dare move his things; when Mother died, I put everything in order in two afternoons, the fourth and fifth day after the funeral. That haste, too, could be explained by the war. Many dead were already filling the newspapers and television screens, and I wanted as soon as possible to flee from every thought of death. I wanted, more precisely said, to stop running from the thought of death, from identifying with death, from the insight into how meaningless a person's life is, but if I closed my eyes, I would hear the voice of the radio announcer, if I plugged my ears, my eyes would fall on the latest newspaper reports, if I fell asleep, I would dream about an endless column of people dressed in rags vanishing over a mountain brink. How long can a person endure with tightly closed eyes or stopped-up ears? How long can he dream? Sooner or later every solution becomes saturated, and death sank through me like sugar through oversweetened water, and just as the sugar settles on the bottom of the glass, so did death flow into my feet. In the evening I stared at my swollen legs; during the day I feared I would no longer be able to move. That's peculiar, I said to Donald; when my father died, it seemed to me that I could take flight, as if death were a trampoline from which I could take off into the air, free of the earth's gravity; when my mother died, I could feel the ground hard under my feet, I walked as if I had been the first person to trek around the world, and while people completely unknown to me were dying in Croatia and Bosnia, death sucked at me as the snake does the mouse, like quicksand. Donald nodded, wrote something in his little pad, and looked at me with those eyes, which I would never have trusted had I been anywhere else. We sat in the restaurant on the island in the river, in the very heart of the city, bent over the map. Our foreheads sometimes touched, especially when we tried to read the names of smaller places, shorter rivers, and huddled mountains. Occasionally my finger slid across borders real and imaginary; occasionally Donald's palm came down on the Adriatic Sea or covered Macedonia. He called my attention to the fact that Croatia looks like gaping jaws, Serbia like a fat prairie dog sitting over its hole, while Bosnia reminded him of a broken triangle, like an unsuccessful triangle, he corrected himself, drawn by the trembling hand of a child. After everything I had told him, he was interpreting the world like a collection of Rorschach inkblots. "After everything that has happened," said Mother, "I'm glad I can still raise my hand to my mouth. When I can no longer raise it, I'll close my eyes and won't open them again. Your father always said that one does not come into the world, that one can only go out of it. At first I believed that this was a sign of a loss of faith; afterward I accepted it as the only thing one can believe in, that there are no comings but only goings, a continual separating, as when you remove the layers from an onion. You don't like onions, but, believe me, love is not everything, and not everything that smells nice is good. I once sang beautifully, but now my voice begins to tremble at the very thought of a song, I don't have to open my mouth. Everything is memory, everything is recollection, though I have always told myself that life is only what is actually lived. You see, your father didn't know how to sing, he didn't have an ear for music worth the dirt under his fingernails, but that's why he knew all the words. He sang to himself, mutely, and I recognized that in him when we met for the first time after the war. I recognized in him the song of mourning that only those whom war has made wrecks of sing. He was never tall, but as I listened to his silent song, I could see how he had once stood upright, how he had known how to walk. My first husband was tall, I had to stand on my toes to lean my head on his upper arm, but when I stood beside your father, I had to stoop down to rest my forehead on his shoulder. He was an emptiness, and I was an emptiness, and we knew we didn't have time enough to fill that which was no longer in us. I hope you will never have to feel that, never have to begin to live from the beginning. I have to drink a little more water." She reached for the glass, then changed her mind. None of that, of course, is heard on the tape, only the squeaking of the little rubber belts grows louder, as if Donald's tape recorder, actually his father's tape recorder, is getting tired and threatening to stop. If I knew how to write, I could make all sorts of things out of that; a real writer would never pass up that network of concurrences, such an opportunity to bring together in a single point the most diverse destinies, to intertwine them and later to unravel them again, and in the fates of people and of things to find that unique thread which holds the weave together and because of which, if it be pulled carelessly, the weave comes apart. Donald was finally getting fed up with my nagging. He moved the beer glasses and cups of coffee to the edge of the table and put both his hands on the map. For the writer, he said, as for nature, there is no conditional mood. Something, he said, either happens or it does not happen; there is no third possibility. Life, he said, is not grammar. Language is a structure that does not exist in the world, he said. His eyes had never been wider than they were now, as he glared at me in the café on the island in the river and beads of perspiration broke out above his upper lip and brows. If you want a story, he said, then first you have to forget about language, is that clear? I asked which language he had in mind. Any, he said, whichever, because all languages say the same thing, only their sounds are different. I wasn't sure if earlier he hadn't said something different, but when I opened my mouth to resist him, he stopped me with an upraised index finger. Then, he said, you do this, and with a quick movement he crumpled the map as if he were picking up a damp tablecloth. I felt like screaming, because as he kneaded the map of my former country, it seemed to me as if he were squashing my own heart. I didn't scream. I glowered at him, and if looks could kill, he would have been dead a long time ago. But the conditional mood, as Donald said, does not exist in nature, and so he still sat there at the table in the restaurant on the island in the river and transformed the map into a paper ball, as I, on the chair opposite him, attempted to bring some order into the confusion that streamed about my body. And now, said Donald, and he put the wretched ball on the table, now you can write. About what, I managed to whisper. About how, between a world of paper and the real world, said Donald, you have chosen the real world. About how, he said, you tried to preserve the world of paper and how you realized, he said, that except for the folds and splits and some tears, there is really nothing in it. As he was saying this, he slowly unraveled the crumpled map and smoothed it out with his hands. And truly, except for the folds, the splits, and two or three tears, nothing on it could be any longer recognized. And in the same way as I had dragged my index finger along roads, borders, and river basins, so now he followed with his the lines along which the fabric of the paper was falling apart. That's your story, said Donald, those fine cracks in which there are no longer color and printer's lead. And now, he said, now we'll each drink one more beer, and then you go home and write; you no longer have any business being here. I turned around. I didn't know anyone in that restaurant, only a table and chair here and there. Even the waitresses had changed at a rhythm faster than the rhythm we had dropped by the restaurant, an uneven rhythm, in fact, faster in the summer and slower in the winter, quite drawn out in the spring, when I had spent my days off in the yard behind the house I lived in and Donald was beginning to hike in the surrounding mountains. What was I to do? I drank up my beer, collected the one-time map of my onetime country, shook hands with Donald, went home, put the rice on to cook, took out a stack of clean sheets of paper, sharpened a pencil, and started to write. My mother would have been disgusted at such behavior. You should never be submissive, she used to say, because life doesn't exist so that someone else can live it for you. But sometimes, as I waited for the silence coming from the tape recording to end, I felt like saying to her that this is the only way one can be alive. "Sometimes," I say aloud, "in order to be what you are, you have to be what you aren't." "Are you still recording?" asks Mother. I probably nodded my head, because I don't hear any reply. "I want to say something else," says Mother. I suppose I nodded again. "I don't believe that life can be told," she said, "still less that it can be written down, though I once read with enjoyment the books *America's First Lady, Marjorie Morningstar, The Young Lions,* and *The Arch of Triumph.* I was still young then, or at least I still believed I was, which is, after all, one and the same thing, but I know now there is not a book into which you can fit an entire life, not even a part of a life. You could write a thousand pages and you wouldn't succeed in recording a part of what happens, for instance, when you thread the eye of a needle. It's silly that I'm talking to you about books, you know about them better than I do, but the whole time I wondered why everything that was happening was happening precisely to me, as when you read a book and wonder why that happened to the main hero, why the heroine was unable to avoid that love affair or whatever else, why she was unable simply to open the door and step outside or at least to go into another room. There are no other rooms; there is no way out of this skin. You can only watch the skin wrinkle as the body shrinks. The skin, in fact, is the one thing you have more of than you need as life goes by; everything else you lack, everything peels away from you like the layers from the onion I spoke of a little while ago, and in the end only the core remains, only the middle, a hotness you can't keep on your tongue too long. Of course, you can think, as I have thought countless times, that everything could have happened differently, that sweetness could have replaced the hotness, but if life could be changed, then we probably wouldn't call it life, we probably wouldn't be alive." I put down the pencil, which I hadn't used to write down anything anyway, and said: "Do you remember that song, sometimes you sang it to us, about the girl who rises early to feed the pigeons and sees that her favorite bird is not there, and remembers that the evening before she saw a hunter going into the forest, and then hearing a shot, and now she knows, as the other pigeons crowd around her feet, for whom the shot had been intended?" Then, by all appearances, it came her turn to nod her head, because now I don't hear her answer. "Perhaps it's always so," I continued, "while we husk corn in the yard, life is being extinguished in some forest." Had I remembered that line earlier, its final part could have been a good title for my book. "Your father always loved that song," said Mother. "And I always thought," I said, "that you sang it to us." Mother again reached for the glass of water, I don't know what else that ringing sound which mingles with the squeaking of little rubber belts and spindles could have been. "It's always so in life," said Mother. "There is always a part that you know and a part that you don't know, and as time goes by, you devote more and more time to thinking about everything you didn't know, as if life, had you found that out, could have been changed." I know exactly what Donald would say if he heard that: He would look me angrily in the face and cry that nothing can be changed, that literature is not engaged in a guessing-game but in a credible description of the facts, regardless of whether they are real or fictional. I had written about that, in a sort of way, with that always-sharpened pencil; afterward I had typed it neatly on an old electric typewriter that I'd bought for twenty dollars at a yard sale in the neighborhood. I had had to change its fuse, to clean it well of dust and oil, and to put in a new ribbon. I'd rubbed it so much that it started to glitter in the dark. And I'd written about a poet who decides the time has come to write stories, but he in no way manages to free himself from concision, which he considers essential to composing verse, and dedicates himself to the interpretations which, so he believes, form the basis of prosaic speech. To him every sentence is still a verse, as every story is still a poem, for form, he realizes, is not important at all. The world around him is falling apart, a war is going on, his mother has died, and he feels, despite all prosaic concision, the story of her life becoming real in him, drawing him into himself and forcing him to play a role determined long ago. I didn't know how to end the story, nor did I know whether it truly was a story, and then I wrote—and it's the only thing I made up—how on the bank of a river he meets a girl to whom he declares in a long monologue that love is the last bastion, and that, if we lose it, life becomes an endless sinking. He's not sure the girl has understood him, which, after all, is not important to him in the least, for he was talking not to her but to himself. On the last page the river slowly rises, and when the poet's monologue is over, they depart trudging through the mud. All of that I wrote in the English language, with the help of a dictionary, of course, though I didn't succeed in finding the best way to handle the verses the poet recites twice, the first time on a balcony, gazing at the starry sky, the second time before he sloshes into the watery mire. The verses were from poems I had written long ago, and which, by the way, no one had wanted to publish. They were full of explosive consonants and long vowels, and that shift of explosions and relaxations, that's what I didn't manage to duplicate in the other language, which was not, of course, important for the story itself, but it aroused in me a feeling of unease and reminded me that life cannot be cut like a meat pie or, a more pet comparison of mine, a chocolate cake. I put the story in an envelope, brought it to the post office, and sent it to Donald. It had been much harder for me to write the cover letter; I probably used more paper for that letter than I had for the entire story. I couldn't get over the thought that Donald is a writer, and thus the tone of the letter constantly skimmed along the alluvia of humility, as if I were appealing to a bureaucrat upon whose decision my entire existence depended. Had she seen it, my mother would have immediately torn it up. For her, openness was the only possible way of existing; she acknowledged nothing else. It's better to talk utter nonsense, she said, than to beat around the bush. In the same way, she never believed those who preached, but those who acted. Whoever knows where he stands, she once said, never asks: Who am I? Many years later, while we were drinking afternoon coffee, she continued that sentence and added that for the person who keeps asking himself who he is, as if someone were continually banging on the door to his soul, no one else exists. For that reason, I suppose, she slept beside Father in an unheated room even though she craved warmth; Father covered himself with a thin quilt, she groaned under a down comforter; Father constantly opened the windows, she stealthily closed them; in winter Father often went bareheaded; she knitted caps that, as the years went by, grew thicker and thicker. She was the first of all of us to go to bed in the evening. In the morning she was the first one on her feet, to start a fire in the kitchen stove, make coffee, prepare breakfast, clean the ashes from the tiled stove, go buy a newspaper. Father was calm, serene as the Buddha; Mother was a live coal, she burned like the eternal flame. So at least I thought when I was a boy and believed the world was unchanging. But when Father died, and she began to fade, even the skin on her hands and cheeks, so I imagined when I would touch or kiss it, was becoming colder. Some ten years after Father's death her eyes had lost their gleam, and I knew that I had nothing left to hope for. I don't know what you were hoping for anyway, Donald would say to that, not trying to hide the trace of malice in his voice. By then, of course, I had learned that the world changes and that the change is lasting, that change, in fact, is the true face of the world, and yet I believed that in that utter transformation there were little islands of immutability, closed systems that resisted every attempt at change. Here Donald would already begin to pity me; he would no longer have a need for malice. When the tanks entered Slovenia, I wanted to shut the door and lower the blinds, to turn off the television and give up the daily press, in order thus, as in some story, to preserve what remained of our family organism. Mother, however, was persistent, pressing the buttons on the remote control and closely following the raised voices of the announcers that hovered over the rapid shift of flickering images. And now I think, as I sit in the house that's not a home, that she had done this with an express purpose, not in order to spite me or to find out what was really happening, for she knew—considering that she had lived through much bloodier conflicts, that in war there is no truth but only adaptable interpretations—but because she had wished to hasten her own end. Just as my father, I'm sure, had decided to die when he realized he could live only as an infirm, crippled body, given to the mercies of other people, so my mother, not wishing to relive her life in a reprise of history, decided to join death. She said to herself: Tomorrow I shall die, and the next day she was dead. She lived, in fact, two days more, but only because contemporary medicine has at its disposal means to extend the pulsations of the organism, to spur the heart as if life were a horse that must win the grand derby. When I visited her in the hospital the day before her death, she was lying on her back, and with right hand held high, forefinger straightened, she pointed to a corner of the room. There it is, she said when I leaned over her. I turned and looked. The corner was empty, not counting a few threads of a cobweb that fluttered on the invisible air currents, as she was empty, not counting the last threads of life that broke and quivered as her soul was lifted to the heights. Here there is no cobweb in the corner, I don't have to turn around. For a brief moment Mother's voice grows louder, as if she had suddenly come closer to the microphone and immediately moved away. "Of course," she said, "life cannot be changed, and the more you try to seize it, the more it slips away." Again she stared at her hands. "When I think of everything that has slipped through these fingers, I could cut them off, but I know that this would bring back nothing. What has once gone, has gone forever. Perhaps I've already said that?" I hear myself saying that she hadn't, but even if she had, I say, it didn't matter. My last words come through quite clearly, as if I'd been leaning over the tape recorder to check how much tape still remained. And now I lean forward and see that both reels are equally filled. With her fingertips Mother touched her temples, eyelids, the corners of her mouth. "I wanted to say something else," she said, "but I no longer remember what." I waited. "Maybe we can continue tomorrow," I suggested, with which Mother silently agreed, but the following day, although I'd prepared everything and Mother had even sat down on the chair opposite the microphone, we didn't succeed in recording a thing. Just when the tape started to turn, someone rang the bell to our front door, and in the next apartment the dog started to bark; Mother rushed to open it and didn't return again to the living room. All of that I now heard: the biting sound of the bell, which all of us always said was too loud, though we never replaced it; the muffled barking; the squeaking of the table Mother had leaned on when she'd gotten up; the unintelligible murmur in the anteroom; the slam of the kitchen door; me clearing my throat. The only thing that wasn't heard was she not returning. I stopped the tape, rewound it, and put it in the red cardboard box, then unplugged the tape recorder, packed the microphone, and rolled up the cables. I carried everything to its place: the tape recorder under the dresser, the accessories in the drawer, the box with the tape on the bookshelf, on which the other tapes were already resting. I returned a little later and pushed all four tapes behind the volumes of the Academy's *Dictionary of the Serbo-Croatian Language*, where they remained for fourteen years. I moved them only once, seven years later, the last time we painted the apartment. At that time I took each book in my hands, dusted it off, and put it in one of the cardboard boxes that for days before I had carried from the butcher shop or the grocery store. When the painting, which always turns out to be an endless project, was finally finished, I returned each book to its old place; I didn't change anything. I suppose that even now, with the exception of the Bible, the two dictionaries, and the illustrated guide across the Rocky Mountains, which I brought to Canada, they're still standing that way, only covered with a layer of new dust. One thing a person learns, at least indirectly, when he goes through the experience of a war: that all of life consists of accumulating objects, regardless of whether they are books, towels, pillowcases, or graphics, as if its meaning lies in the fact that we build our very own museums, which sooner or later, and particularly at the moment when departing becomes inevitable, turn into collections of useless things. It was because of this, I'm sure, that I cleared out all of Mother's things so quickly, and only five or six days after her funeral nothing in the apartment any longer betrayed her presence. When Father died, we had weighed each of his things, first in our right and then in our left hand, as if our continued existence had depended upon every one of them. Upon Mother's things nothing depended. The country was falling apart, I was falling apart, memories were the ballast that pulled one violently toward bottom. At that time, while stuffing her things into plastic bags and large cardboard boxes that had once held crackers and meat chops, I found the letters from her first husband and a roll of bank notes from the Kingdom of Yugoslavia. The bank notes I gave to the boy in the next building to whom I'd earlier also given postage stamps and coins brought from my trips to foreign countries. The letters I read. The man who had written them knew he was going to die, though he tried hard not to admit that to himself and mentioned the "imminent transport" that was supposed to take them to "some far-off land," on forced labor. It took them to some little wood outside Belgrade, where, mowed down by machine gun bullets, they fell into soil much nearer and more real, into holes they had most likely dug themselves beforehand. I didn't know whether that agreed with historical fact, but I could imagine how at that very moment, as I read, similar transports were moving toward similar little woods in some other part of my country. The weapons had changed since then, they had become lighter and more rapid, but the tools for digging the earth had remained the same: the spade and the shovel, sometimes the pickax or bare human fingers. None of this had been written in those letters; even had he known something, Mother's first husband surely wouldn't have dared write it; what he did know, however, was his love. Had they not arrived from the camp, some sentences could be thought as having been written from a great distance, perhaps from a business trip that was just about to end. Later, concern replaces love, he is anxious at the fate of his wife and children, he believes the course of fate can still be changed.

There are parts in which he painfully laments over himself, but also sentences in which he shifts part of the blame to his wife for the state he found himself in. Had they, when they abandoned Zagreb, remained in Bosnia, none of that, he was convinced, would be happening to them. He didn't know, he couldn't have known, that the Bosnian Jews had perished along with all the other Jews from the territory of the Independent State of Croatia, most often in the Ustashe camps, which was really the only difference, because the camp he was in had been run by the Germans. The last letter bore the date 14 November 1941. In it he wrote, almost with the relief of a man who has had enough of worrying over his own fate, that the moment had finally arrived for his transport. Perhaps the very next day, he wrote, he would be going somewhere far away, he didn't know where, but he was deeply convinced that nothing, no distance and no event, would yet keep them apart. If, in case, she were to receive a suitcase with his things later on, there was no need to worry, because many were leaving that way, without anything, because there, where they were going, they were being told that none of that would be needed. After all, he wrote, he had never been afraid of work, so why would he be afraid of more work, no matter how tiring it was. And then he wrote: Know it is my wish that my sons be raised as Serbs and by no means as Jews. The words "by no means" had been underlined with a thick wavy line. I couldn't believe my eyes. The paper fell from my hand, and when I bent down to pick it up, I struck my forehead on the edge of the table. I read that sentence again. How great had the despair in that man been that he could have thought upbringing is stronger than fate? I tried to picture my mother sitting in some dimly lit room and bending over that letter, in the same way as I was bending over it, the pain deepening in my frontal bone and eating away her heart. She would never have done that, I knew, because so many times before she had changed her being precisely in order to preserve the Jewish faith of those children, in the same way that, after the war, she had again changed her being in order to instill Judaism in her new children, in my sister and me. I wasn't sure I had completely understood that, but I was able to get some idea of the burden she had had to carry within herself on account of it. Having refused his last wish, she had also renounced him; having again chosen a Jew for a husband, she had overcome the evil that had previously overcome him and made him loathe himself. In the final outcome, however, she had betrayed him, though neither before nor after did she betray anyone, and that fact always stood beside her like a shadow. Why, then, hadn't she destroyed those letters? I could no longer ask her. My life had suddenly become an answer to the life of a man whom I had never seen; I existed in order that he, despite the difficult-to-comprehend idea of universal annihilation, could continue to exist. I gathered the letters and carefully folded them along the same worn-out creases, then put them back in the yellowish envelope, the same one in which they had abided in Mother's purse. The paper had crumbled; the table was covered with whitish particles; had I been able to view them under a microscope, had I only had a microscope, who knows what fantastic forms I would have seen. I was trembling, my face was beaded with perspiration, nausea was beginning to rush from my stomach, and that night, for the first time since Mother's death, I felt fear at being alone in the apartment. I stared with eyes wide open at the darkness above the couch I lay on and at the shadows that flitted across the room each time a car or truck passed along the street. At times I have imagined that one benefit of a parent's death can be found in the fact that afterward a man stops being someone's son and that, at least for a while, he walks as if the world belongs to him alone, but then, as the blanket smothered me and the pillowcase clung to my neck, I feared that same solitude to which I had once ascribed magnificence and which, the darkness told me, was all I had left. I never told this to Donald. I never, of course, told this to anyone. Nor did I have anyone to tell. The war went on, money lost its worth, people changed, words became more and more empty. Only my fear remained the same. I would put off going to bed until my head drooped or the book fell from my hand, and then, as soon as I lay down and turned off the light, my eyes would bulge and I'd stare into the darkness out of which something constantly flew at me. Nothing, in truth, ever reached me; fear, after all, is not actuality; fear is the threat of actuality, the possibility that something is occurring. In vain did I repeat this to myself, and in vain I left the table lamps lighted. I always saw that same void Mother's first husband had seen the night before the departure of his transport, of that sadly short journey to the place where a dug-out grave already awaited them. Everything else that happened after that I can now, as I sit beside the table on which the tape recorder is lying like a fresh corpse, sum up in one long sentence. Attempting to flee from my fear, despair, and pain, I sought salvation by sinking into a fear, despair, and pain greater than my own, and so I accepted an offer to work in the office of one of the international humanitarian organizations, responsible for distributing aid and collecting data regarding refugees, which required me constantly to meet with those whose misfortune was not symbolic like my own, to help elderly women step across thresholds, to guide trembling hands toward the lines on forms which had been designated for their personal signatures, to regard the eyes of children that never, no matter how long you looked at them, blinked, as though something had left them open forever, and then I began to visit the refugee camps, to take and record statements, to inventory lost and destroyed property, to make lists of the lost and missing or those who had simply been forgotten, to stack piles of almost worthless money toward which fingers with cracked fingernails reached, to find a doll for a little girl who couldn't remember her own name, diapers for babies, medicines for the chronically ill, to translate and interpret, describe and summarize, until the moment I felt I couldn't feel anything anymore and that someone else's fear of a lost and changing world had canceled my fear of a repeating one. Then I left on my trip. Not immediately afterward, of course, but now I'm rushing with that account, because my glance at the square wall clock tells me that soon I can expect Donald to arrive. He called me when he received my parcel, he still hadn't opened it, and suggested that he visit me the following Saturday, that is, today, a little after ten in the evening, as soon as he'd finished exercising in the weight room and swimming in the pool. His voice had sounded indifferent. I don't know why I expected it should have sounded otherwise; perhaps because mine had trembled as I answered his questions and because I had hopelessly muddled the simplest grammatical constructions of a language I already considered my own. We exchanged a few more words about trivial things, about beer and the weather, and then he became furious when I chided him for so easily acquiescing to Quebec's demand to secede, which, I emphasized, irresistibly reminded me of the beginning of the breakup of my former country. We're not such barbarians, Donald snapped. My mother was right, I thought, one should never believe people in whose eyes nothing is seen. Afterward we again spoke amiably, Donald asked me to jot down the day and time of his arrival, and then we, first he and then I, hung up. That slip of paper even now hangs on the refrigerator, lost in that profusion of messages, want ads, and instructions for the recycling of paper, newsprint, cans, and cardboard materials. As I'd been writing it out, I thought of writing one more, a reminder to explain to Donald what the mud through which the poet and the girl slosh at the end of my story really signifies, but I quickly gave up on the idea. Had I wanted to explain, then I wouldn't have written it; if I'd written it, then there'd be no need to explain. Be that as it may, when on the appointed Saturday, this morning, I woke up, the mud didn't even cross my mind. I felt anxious, of that I'm sure. Had I stood up, I don't doubt my knees would have begun to buckle, the same way they used to shake when on the deserted streets of Zemun, late at night, I would encounter the police. And so, in order to overcome my disquiet, I decided to listen to the tapes of Mother's confession. I had tried to do that several times before, the first time on the day I brought the tape recorder from Donald's basement, but not once did I succeed in getting myself to be that patient. At first the squeaking of the little rubber belts and loose spindles got on my nerves, then I suspected I had rearranged the order of the tapes; on one occasion I started to cry and my lungs began to hurt from the violent sobs, and the whole time I was tormented by the fear that a return to my native language, reinforced by the fact that it was precisely my mother who was speaking it, would bring me back to where I no longer wanted to return, especially now that, thanks to someone else's language, I was finally beginning to feel like someone else. There are those, both here and there, who would say that this is a cause for shame rather than a sign of complete fulfillment, but I am comforted by the thought that my mother would not have said that. Only those who have forced you to think about shame, she would say, should be ashamed. I don't know what Donald would say. He'd probably say nothing or write something down in his little pad. If he were to do that, he'd hide the page he's writing on with his left hand, frown, and lick his lips. His hand and the lip licking didn't bother me, but on every such occasion I wanted to put my palm on his forehead and smooth out the wrinkles, because writing, I wished to tell him, should always be connected with joy, even when it's a question of a difficult verse or a hopelessly complicated sentence. I never did that. I knew, that is, the astonishment with which he would have looked at me had I touched so much as a hair on his head, let alone his skin. Perhaps he would even have fallen off his chair or overturned a glass of beer. Horrible is the touch of the human hand. So goes one of my verses, perhaps the title of one of my poems. At that time I was unable to suppose that soon after Father's death I would think of how he and I had never touched each other. The hugging fell to Mother; he always remained beyond the range of touch. Mother was quick to oblige; he waited to be approached. Mother knew when to speak aloud, when to whisper, when to coo; he constantly spoke in the same voice, as if there weren't any differences between the words. Perhaps I could tell all this to Donald when he arrives instead of telling only myself. In any case, I should tell him what I heard on Mother's tapes, not in its entirety, of course, not everything, but yet in greater detail, if he has that much time, that much patience to listen. I get up, go to the window, listen attentively. The tapes are lying on the table, each in its own protective cardboard box. If I don't count the books I brought, the tapes are the only proof of my existence in time; a voice which is no longer a voice, from the beyond and absent, only a mechanical exchange of realities, confirms my presence; I am here thanks to the one who is not here. I suppose that now, after having listened to the tapes, I can pack them and send them to Belgrade. I would still be left with only the books, but it's easy to free oneself from books, both sacred and profane; never yet have books posed an insuperable obstacle. Perhaps I'm rushing; perhaps I'd do better to go into the kitchen, wash a cup and saucer, wipe the tablecloth, look over the messages on the refrigerator door. In only one way can someone wait, said my mother, and that is not to wait. And while all of us paced from door to window, craned our necks, and peered out at dawn or in the early evening, she found something to do in the kitchen, cleaned a carrot or young peas, chopped an onion, scrubbed a pot, kneaded dough. She achieved complete serenity by copying recipes from newspapers and clippings into her culinary notebook. Again I sit down, again I get up, again I go to the window, again I listen attentively. All this is unnecessary, of course, since Donald is coming with his car, which means, keeping in mind the quiet that reigns in the area I live in, that I'll hear him as soon as he turns off the main road. When he arrives, refreshed from swimming in the pool and his strength gathered in the weight room, it will be a very appropriate ending to the day, crammed with symbolic meaning, particularly for someone who, like me, has spent it in an uninterrupted free fall down the cliffs of memory while the strength has leaked from him as if it were a body fluid. Even someone who doesn't know how to write can understand this, can draw lines that from opposite directions hurtle toward the point of intersection, one that records loss and decline, the other that designates renewal and recovery, to that same place where they are joined by the spiral of memory, which leads downward, and the spiral of self-confidence, which leads nowhere, though Donald would become livid with anger because of that remark. Hence at that point of intersection everything ends and, at the same instant, everything begins. Even someone who doesn't know how to write can see that here the world turns into text, that sights become letters, that silence is transformed into the whiteness of a page. One life, symbolically and practically, ends on the same day on which, symbolically and practically, a new life begins. Exit Mother and enter Donald; that's how it would be written in a play if all this were a stage performance and not real life. Somewhere a door closes, somewhere another one opens, the light begins to flood in, for a brief moment the entire scene is bathed in radiance, and then, considerably later, the curtain falls. That reminds me to draw back the curtain on my window, because Donald, seeing the light turned down, may think I've fallen asleep. Never, in fact, have I been more awake, more prepared for what is about to happen, for that which—it's better I say it this way—must happen. My mother would have surely objected. Never, not for the world, put everything into one person's hands, she said, always keep a part for yourself. I don't know on which occasion she said that, and perhaps she even hadn't been addressing herself to me, but to my sister, but that's not important. I've already put everything into Donald's hands, and when I say this, I really do mean everything; nothing remains, least of all the part Mother spoke of, for I've offered Donald not only pages of a story but also everything that may happen after that story if, of course, he accepts what I have written. I have relinquished an entire possible life into his hands, and in the fact that Donald is coming to my house after the swimming and exercising, I find a confirmation of his desire to hold on to everything I've offered him still more tenaciously. I can understand my mother's caution and I don't doubt I would have acted in the same way had I been in her place, but I'm not in her place, I'm not, in fact, in any place, and perhaps, when I speak about a possible life, I am really speaking about place, about a life that becomes place. A life without place is a mere flitting about. I don't know who said that; certainly not my mother, regardless of the fact that she lived her life precisely as if it were place. Wherever she found herself, there she belonged; I wouldn't be able to say that about myself. If I knew how to write better, I could make a story from those differences, a history written in apparently contradictory fragments, united by the same sense of loss, such that at the end every going away is transformed into a drawing near. I'm rushing again, of course, and already I'm speaking about the possibility of writing better, but I still don't know if I know how to write at all. Soon I'll begin to peer through the window again, open the door; maybe I'll even go to the edge of the pavement, maybe I'll sit on the grass. It would be better, though, if I washed a cup and saucer, picked up the things that are lying about, tightened the blanket on the bed. Donald, I'm sure, doesn't like disorder. If this is true, then there's something in common between him and my mother. As soon as she opened the door to some room or the kitchen, she would head straight for a forgotten item, an ashtray with cigarette butts, a plate with apple peels, untouched dust, a smudge on a windowpane. Nothing escaped her view, her touch, her concern. She was the only one about whom no one dared worry. She became angry because of our attempts to explain her pallor or the dark circles under her eyes. She poured the boiling water into the hot-water bottle herself, made teas, massaged her joints, prepared compresses of brandy and onions. In the morning she was again the first one on her feet, to light a fire in the stove and then go shopping. The night was for illness; the day had to remain the same. I've endured enough lives already, said Mother, I can't begin yet another one. The first part of that sentence I had used as the opening line of a poem about an old woman who sits on a bench beside the trunk of a cherry tree, although the rest of the poem is different and doesn't offer even the possibility of the existence of a new life. And the beginning is really different, too, considering that it doesn't emphasize, as in Mother's case, a sufficiently large number of lives endured, but rather its quantity, its sufficiency of extent. In any event, even if between those two meanings there is no essential difference, the old woman in the poem knew that there, where she was, the end has no beginning. The end is the end. I can only surmise what Donald would say about this kind of message from a literary work, but I was young enough then to believe in some other things, for instance, in the salutary effect of freeing oneself from fear and death. The fact that I hadn't written my poem in the first person but had instead put it in the old woman's mouth, of course, says something about me, perhaps more than does the poem itself. My face could be read, Mother claimed, like a book written in boldface letters. It probably can be read the same way now, only the letters have become tinier and their meaning less accessible, particularly in this country, where facial expression is less important than words and the mouth says more than the eye. It's not important how one sees but how one talks, and whoever doesn't know how to talk is blind. That's a modest conclusion, nothing special, but little insights still bring me great joy, because of which Donald, the first time I mentioned this to him, couldn't hide his surprise. According to him, the European, as well as the American, is incapable of seeing beauty and grandeur in the small; only a person from the East is able to do something like that; the European, to be sure, finds beauty in the harmonious relationship of large forms, while the American needs nothing but largeness itself; in the East a point has cosmic dimensions, while in the West there is form but without features. Whoever in North America doesn't believe in largeness, said Donald, has no business being here. On that occasion, too, we were sitting in the restaurant on the island in the river and emptying pitchers of beer, while around us the city rose from all sides. Now I'm no longer sure whether that was at the beginning of our acquaintanceship or if it occurred later, but even had I kept a diary or at least an orderly chronology, that would change nothing. Words do not exist in time; they're spoken or they're not spoken; that is all; there is no third possibility. Even when they're recorded on tape recorder tape, they don't exist in the past but only at the moment someone decides to listen to them again, enables them to speak again, at least by means of electronics, plastics, and magnetic currents. Even then, however, they will not speak out of a more or less defined segment of the past but will always be acknowledged in a new opening in the present, which means, of course, that they will never be the same since all the parameters that define any moment in the present cannot be repeated twice. Perhaps, I think, I shouldn't send the tapes of Mother's voice back to Belgrade? Perhaps it would be more useful to hold on to them and, when all of this is over, and even before, to listen to them one more time, even many times? If I had a pencil and a scrap of paper handy, I wouldn't neglect to write that down and fasten it to my refrigerator among the other slips of paper. Mother, of course, would have been disgusted had she seen that forest of messages: What you can do today, she constantly repeated, don't leave for tomorrow. And she never left anything. It took me a long time to free myself from the unease the finality of that sentence had caused in me, for in spite of all my efforts, I was unable to talk myself into being so orderly. I got up at the same time, I went to bed at the same time, I kept a meticulous journal, but something always spilled over the rim of the day, something always remained for tomorrow or, more often, for the day after tomorrow, especially when I passed from one week to another or when one month would end and a new one begin. To be sure, all of that became irrelevant when I deprived myself of the journal and began to leave messages on the refrigerator door. All in all, I think as I stare through the kitchen window into the ever-thickening darkness, it is quite certain that I am no longer he who I once was, as it is certain that, after Donald's arrival, I shall never again be he who I am now. Once the line is drawn, said my mother, you can do only two things, add or subtract; there is no longer any cheating. I abruptly rise on tiptoe, listen attentively, but quickly recognize the sound of my neighbor's car. Donald, then, is still on the way. Mother, however, was right: Life must always be lived from the beginning; you may keep in your pocket a handful of photographs, but that is all, there is no looking back, no comparing, no searching for similarities and differences. Nothing is similar, nothing is different. Each thing is a thing unto itself, just as each person is a type unto himself, a set of singularities and not a sum of samenesses. If my mother had erred in something, which I see quite clearly now, as if she herself had stated it in the recorded tapes, she had erred in believing in the necessity of place; life perhaps is a planted egg, she thought, but the nest must always be the same. Though this choice of words may remind one of her bent for proverbs and folk wisdom, she surely wouldn't have said it that way. That's not important now; nothing is important anymore, especially if I don't count the dirty dishes in the sink. When we were recording the tapes in Zemun, I was bewitched by Father's death and believed that, if I got Mother to speak about her life, I would be better prepared to receive her death. When she died, I realized that no kind of preparation helps: Death is always unexpected, perhaps most of all when it is patiently waited for. Father had raved in his bed, thrown off the bedding, torn his underwear, while Mother lay quite peacefully, sometimes even raising her head from the pillow or her arms, as at the very end. One might be able to say because of this that Father had fought for additional life and that Mother had reconciled with death; in reality, of course, Father had invited death and Mother had despaired at losing life. In all of that, Donald, clearly, wouldn't fail to note the symbolic coincidence of Mother's whirled fate and the political fate of my country, but regardless of the attractiveness of such an interpretation, I am more of the opinion that Mother had had no other choice, that she had simply repeated what had been written into the space around her, just as the hero of my story had had to repeat it, if indeed it is a story. I know that now, as I stand here in this little kitchen, but I didn't know that then, while, beneath the old-fashioned chandelier in the living room of our Zemun apartment, I tried to douse the jealousy that arose in me as I listened to Mother's story. Had I remained there, it seems to me that I once told this to Donald, I would have been sucked in like a tiny crumb. I didn't say what would have sucked me in, and I don't know that even now. Donald didn't ask; if he was thinking of something, then he was thinking of a tornado, he'd never in his life seen any other kind of whirlwind, perhaps only some whirlpool in a mountain river. And had I wanted to explain to him the force with which the maelstrom of history had pulled into itself, he would have understood nothing. History had for him been really a textbook, a handbook about events which, once having occurred, as the authors claimed, could no longer be repeated. The fact that my mother had walked a little bent over, as if she were constantly climbing a steep slope, as if she were resisting something that was pulling her downward, they would have attributed to rheumatism and not to historical reality. Donald, probably, hadn't thought any differently, despite all my efforts, despite the coffee, the beer, the maps, and the slowpoke waitresses in the restaurant on the island in the river. People, in truth, are not interested in the sum total of events that make up the individual person; for all of them, destiny is a common trait; we are like spikes of grain or a school of fish, even if someone is attacked by a fungus or caught on a hook, these are only confirmations of the similarities and not proofs of the differences. I stare into the darkness, prick up my ears, and list in my mind everything my mother had known how to do: to transplant, for instance, every flower at the right moment into a flowerpot of the right size; to curdle unripened cheese; to light a fire in the kitchen stove and carry the live coals to the tiled stove in the living room; to make a mixture of garlic, wine vinegar, and pork fat rinsed nine times in water which, when rubbed on the entire body, brought down the highest temperature and drew out the highest fever; to make use of every swatch of cloth and bit of thread, every coil of wire, every cardboard or plastic box; to make a front out of a back; to knit, crochet, and embroider; to play solitaire; to polish the parquet floor using a rag sprinkled with paraffin; to make a sodium bicarbonate solution to gargle the throat; to sift flour through a fine sieve; to darn a sock stretched over a wooden darning egg; to fold a pita filled with greens; to butcher a chicken; to separate the white from the yolk; to whip cream. None of that do I know how to repeat. I don't even know how to remain silent in the way she remained silent, her lips pressed gently together, her left hand shading her eyes. She was always afraid her eyes would fail her; the joints and then the eyes, that had been the order of her fears; there is nothing more terrible, she said, than to be immobile in constant darkness. I don't remember exactly what the doctors wrote on her death certificate, but not one of those Latin words was sufficiently convincing. I think they mentioned the heart, perhaps the lungs and kidneys, perhaps distended veins, the usual things for a usual death, as if there are two identical deaths, as if dying doesn't represent an act of the highest distinction, as if in death a person doesn't become what he truly is, what no one else can be. When Mother died, a part of me died with her, just as one part of her had died along with my father, a second with the children from her previous marriage, a third with her first husband, and as the rabbi spoke the prayers and the gravediggers waited behind the mound of freshly dug earth, leaning on the handles of their shovels, I could think of nothing other but those minor deaths, those minor but dependable estrangements from the world, and I thought of how I would go to a place where my death will hurt no one, where everyone will remain whole. By then the war had become a monotonous, everyday affair; one read the news in the daily papers with the same attention as the regular installments of the comic strips, the results of sports matches, and the columns with oddities from all corners of the globe. My mother's passing had interested no one. No one, in truth, was any longer interested in anything, for everything, despite our will, was happening anyhow; even words were turning into predictable refrains or, at best, into a variation which, tangled in itself, succeeded in saying nothing more than we already knew beforehand. I no longer had a country, I was left without a mother, it only remained for language to be completely worn out and for me to remain without anything. Then I left. Even to me it now seems that all of this happened very quickly, though in reality it had lasted much longer: Two years had passed since the moment I'd thrown a handful of earth on Mother's coffin and the time my departure had actually taken place. Everything, in fact, had gone slowly, almost endlessly, especially on the nights I was getting used to her absence. All I had done quickly was to part with her things; I hadn't, as I'd once done with Father's, moved them from dresser to dresser, hadn't weighed them first in one and then the other hand, imagining I could find some new, sometimes exalted, purpose for them. The things no longer meant anything to me, which caused me additional pains in my work with the refugees, because they talked almost exclusively of things, as if all of life could be reduced to a sum of possessions and a balance of losses, and the moment I realized that, I knew I had begun to approach something else. I wasn't sure, it's true, what that was, just as I didn't know which direction I ought to go in and what I ought to approach, but when the place from which a person moves away and according to which he reckons his position in the universe no longer exists, then every direction is equally good. I once tried to explain all this to Donald, not in those words and perhaps not so pithily, but the essence had been the same. A mother, of course, cannot be replaced, but a country and a language— why not? Only in that way, I said, can I cease being someone else's guaranty, debt, or last will and testament, and even, if I desire, memory. Donald looked at me with a sad look, the one that appeared in his eyes after the third beer. I explained no further, but when I was putting the story in the envelope, I remembered his unfocused stare and for a moment I stopped. It was too late, both then and now. I long ago forsook my mother's advice according to which you shouldn't rely on others if you can't rely on yourself, and the only thing left for me to do is to stare into the darkness and explain the noises that are coming from the street behind my yard. The silence then descends on the soiled dishes, in the same way as the invisible motes of dust adhere to the cardboard boxes with the tape recordings or the beads of perspiration cling to my upper lip. As I dust them off, I hear the sound of an automobile entering our street and stopping in front of my house. Shack is a better word for it. Whoever writes, whoever wants to write, must always bear in mind that a word may be spoken only once; if one errs then, nothing can be done about it. I could perhaps rush off to the window in the living room and peep outside, but I stay where I am. When I look up at the square wall clock I see the big hand, with an awkward twitch, pass to the next minute. Then I hear a car door slamming, then the quiet patter of footsteps on the concrete walk that leads to the three steps before the entrance to my little house. I don't hear the last three footsteps, but I imagine Donald ascending, refreshed, smiling, his index finger already pointing in the direction of the doorbell on the left side of the door frame. And when I in fact hear the bell, I don't hesitate but I don't hurry either. I breathe in the air as if it is quite different air, as if these are no longer my lungs, as if this is no longer I. That's how, I say to myself, fruit feels before the blender turns it into juice, how the egg white fears before the whisk transforms it into meringue. Mother would have surely been proud of these culinary comparisons, even if she knew they indicate a transformation into something else. Into someone else, I think and open the front door. Donald stands before it, as I had imagined, but there's no smile on his face. Nor are there the freshness and relaxation I had expected: his face is hard, his shoulders hunched, his feet planted firmly on the ground. I ascribe this to the fact that he has remained on the second step and that now for the first time I am seeing him from that angle, but when he hands me a folder containing a manuscript, his arm begins to shake as though he were lifting one of my suitcases. The manuscript, I see as I casually leaf through it, is full of corrections, places that are underlined, and crossed-out words, I notice a string of big question marks. I close the folder and move aside; Donald, however, remains in the same spot. I, too, could perhaps return to my previous spot, but I can't determine where I was standing. The darkness behind Donald's back is thicker than the dusk that covers the sky and through which a flash of blueness here and there still breaks. If I really knew how to write, if I only had a scrap of paper and a lead pencil, I could make a note of our motionlessness and recognize in it the announcement of a change, the moment when the heart decides to leap into ruin. Then the blueness disappears, the door frame fills with darkness, and when I try to close the door, I feel the darkness resist. I press against it with my shoulder, I shove my foot beneath it, I lean my whole body on its smooth upper surface. The lock finally clicks. Then cautiously, quite cautiously, I move rearward until something touches me in the back.

■ □ ■ □ ■

ABOUT THE AUTHOR

David Albahari was born in 1948 in the Serbian village of Peć.
He is the founder and was for many years the editor in chief of
Pismo, a magazine of world literature. He is also an accom-
plished translator of Anglo-American literature. His works
include *Words Are Something Else,* a short-story collection, and
Tsing, a novel, both published by Northwestern University
Press. He lives in Calgary, Alberta.

■ □ ■ □ ■

WRITINGS FROM AN UNBOUND EUROPE

Bait
Tsing
Words Are Something Else
DAVID ALBAHARI

City of Ash
EUGENIJUS ALIŠANKA

Skinswaps
ANDREJ BLATNIK

My Family's Role in the World Revolution and Other Prose
BORA ĆOSIĆ

Peltse and Pentameron
VOLODYMYR DIBROVA

The Victory
HENRYK GRYNBERG

The Tango Player
CHRISTOPH HEIN

A Bohemian Youth
JOSEF HIRŠAL

Charon's Ferry
GYULA ILLYÉS

Mocking Desire
Northern Lights
DRAGO JANČAR

Balkan Blues: Writing Out of Yugoslavia
JOANNA LABON, ED.

The Loss
VLADIMIR MAKANIN